Priceless Kiss

Priceless
Book 1

Roxy Sloane

Roxy Sloane Books

Also by Roxy Sloane:

THE SEDUCTION SERIES:

Note to readers:

This book is dark, spicy, and contains vengeful women, dominant men, and all kinds of deliciously explicit scenes.

There is also brief discussion of suicide and self-harm (although those themes are not directly depicted in the 'on-screen' action), so if you find the topics distressing, here's your prior warning.

For the academic overachievers who grew up to crave a different kind of praise...
I see you ;)

Priceless: Book One

Priceless Kiss

Vengeance is priceless... Discover the spicy, thrilling new saga from USA Today bestselling author Roxy Sloane!

Sebastian Wolfe is a billionaire hedge fund owner, adored and feared across the globe.

Untouchable. Or so he thinks.

I was prepared to give everything I have to make him pay for his crimes.

My innocence. My body.

My life.

But it turns out, to have my revenge, he'll demand the one thing I can never let him take:

My *heart*.

THE PRICELESS TRILOGY:

1. Priceless Kiss (Sebastian & Avery)

2. Priceless Secret (Sebastian & Avery)

3. Priceless Fate (Sebastian & Avery)

Chapter 1

Avery

Revenge.

They say it will drive a man out of his mind. But what about a woman? We're supposed to be the fairer sex. Gentle.

Forgiving.

Whoever said that must have been a fool, because there's nothing gentle about the fury pounding in my veins as I approach the front steps of the Hotel du Cap, the most luxurious location in the South of France. It's like something from a fairytale, where doormen in brocade vests tip their caps respectfully, and the lobby glitters with ornate chandeliers. The scent of fresh jasmine beckoning me to the back terrace with its stunning views of the manicured lawns and ocean beyond.

It's a long way from Hell's Kitchen, that's for sure. But I'm not here for a vacation.

"You don't have to do this, Avery." My companion murmurs beside me. Nero Barretti, head of the most feared mafia organization in New York. I've known him since I was a kid, and he's like a brother to me.

The only person who could understand what's brought me here tonight.

"Love's making you soft," I reply, darting a glance around the lobby. He cut his honeymoon short to be here with me, but as much as I appreciate the moral support, I don't need a friend right now. I need a coconspirator: the deadly mob boss with blood-stained hands and a heart of stone.

The man who understands what it means to make someone pay.

"Come on." Nero tries again. "What do you say we call Lily, hop a flight to Paris, and drink champagne at midnight under the Eiffel Tower? You know she'd love to see you."

For a moment, I try to imagine it. Turning my back on this crazy vendetta of mine to go take a trip with my friends, trying to forget my broken heart by playing tourist instead of preparing myself for battle.

But the picture stays murky. I can't even imagine it, that's how deep in this I already am. *Fun* is a foreign word to me now. I'm not capable of smiles or laughter or any good times.

The only pleasure I'll know is the day I wreak my revenge.

"I'm not changing my mind." I say firmly. "You, more than anyone, should know why."

Nero must see the steely determination in my eyes, because he gives a nod. His expression shifts, all business again. "The invite said they'll be in the private villa."

I tuck my arm through his and take a deep breath. "Let's go."

A staff member escorts us through the manicured gardens, to a rose-colored villa tucked far away from the main hotel. As if the guests are too wealthy and private to even mix with the other five-star clientele.

"Did your guy finish scrubbing my records?" I ask softly as we walk.

Nero nods. "There's no trace of your old identity anywhere online. I had a guy plant fake papers at City Hall. Your cover will stand up if anyone goes digging around."

"And you know the part you're playing tonight?"

"Cocky asshole with a short fuse?" Nero says with a smirk.

I try to swallow back my nerves. "It's not a joke. If anyone suspects, even for a moment—"

"I know." He cuts me off. "Don't worry. I know the stakes." He pauses, then adds quietly, "Miles was my friend, too."

The name sends a shudder through my body, but I hold it back. I can't let his memory distract me or make me weak.

No, I need it to keep fuelling me instead. It's brought me this far, halfway across the world with a furious vengeance pounding in my chest. Planning a fate that would have been unthinkable to me just a few short weeks ago.

But it's funny what grief can do.

"Mr. Barretti." A man in an expensive suit greets us at the door. "Welcome to the game."

Nero nods and leads me inside the villa. It's lavishly appointed, all gilt and antique furnishings. And the people here tonight... They're just as luxurious. Fresh off the multi-million-dollar yachts anchored down in the bay, the men casually sporting designer watches on their tanned wrists as they take their seats at the card table, while the women sip champagne and glance sharply at every new arrival.

At *me*.

Panic strikes in my chest. I'm way out of my league. What made me think I could not only blend with these people, but stand out in the crowd?

Breathe, I tell myself.

It's not me on display tonight. Not really.

I check my reflection in one of the ornate mirrors, and I'm shocked to find I don't even recognize the woman staring back at me. I've spent my life dressing for comfort, for defense. Heavy boots to run and kick; leather and denim, thick eyeliner, a 'Don't fuck with me' glare. Growing up in the Barretti crime world, I learned fast how to take care of myself, using my clothes and makeup to say I wasn't one of the girls they passed around for fun, or a hot fling on a Friday night.

And if that didn't get the message across, the switchblade in my pocket would.

But tonight, there's nothing harsh or threatening about me.

My hair falls in soft waves around a face that feels naked, even though I'm wearing layers of subtle makeup. Pale shimmer on my eyelids, a gentle blush on my cheeks. I'm fresh-faced and wide-eyed, with just a hint of mascara and pink lip gloss. And my dress...?

It's white. Pristine. Swooping off my shoulders in a modest sweetheart neckline, silk petals breezing in a floaty skirt around my bare thighs—a far cry from all the showstopping skin-tight numbers here tonight. My strappy sandals are delicate, fastened at the ankles with jewel-encrusted straps that match the simple diamond bracelet hanging off one wrist.

The effect is startling. I seem innocent. Young. *Expensive.*

I look like a stranger. The old Avery is gone.

But maybe it's better this way, I decide, turning away from the mirror. Because that version of myself turned to ashes the moment the man I love took his own life, trapped in guilt and shame over his gambling debts.

Debts held by one man.

Him.

Heads turn as Sebastian Wolfe strolls into the villa. Not with revulsion or hatred like he deserves, but excitement. Awe.

Desire.

I stare, taking him in. It's hard to believe this is the first time I've laid eyes on the man in person when he's consumed every waking thought of mine for weeks. But I can tell that the photos online don't do him justice. They can't capture the arrogant edge to his icy blue-eyed stare, or the way his perfectly tailored suit drapes over his lean, 6'2" frame as he saunters through the room. It's not just his wealth on display, but his confidence, too. He's a grown man, twelve years older than me, radiating power and dominance. Every inch an apex predator. The top of any food chain.

But even the deadliest animals can be brought down with a well-timed shot to the heart.

My resolve hardens, and my grip on Nero must have too, because he squeezes my hand in comfort—and warning.

"Welcome, everyone." Sebastian says, in a cut-glass English accent. He looks around the villa like he owns it. Which, I guess he does, since he's picking up the tab for this little get-together. "I won't bore you with the formalities, you all know the rules. Bates here will collect your proof of funds as your entry pass, and we can get the game started. Let's have some fun."

There's applause and laughter, but I feel my fury rising, just being in the same room as the man.

"Easy," Nero murmurs. "Remember, this is only the beginning."

He's right. All great journeys begin with a single step. And so, I force myself to take a glass of champagne, and follow Nero to the card table. My eyes down, demure. Nervous. But inside, I've never been more determined of anything.

Because I made a vow, the day I found Miles' body swinging from the rafters. I'm going to destroy Sebastian Wolfe's life.

The way he's destroyed mine.

Chapter 2

Avery

The high rollers take their seats at the table, and the rest of us settle in to watch. I perch on a chair just behind Nero, positioned directly across from Sebastian's seat, so I'll be directly in his eyeline. He's still circulating, shaking hands and greeting friends, and I force myself not to look at him.

Because now comes the real test. My dress, the makeup, the wide-eyed way I'm glancing around the room, it's all designed with one purpose in mind.

To make him want me.

As a lover, as a plaything... I don't care. But from everything I've managed to learn about Sebastian Wolfe, I know one thing matters most of all to him. Winning. Taking what other men prize, just to watch them lose it.

And he wants to beat Nero more than anything.

They've been locked in a battle of wills for the better part of a year now, ever since Nero intervened with his hostile takeover of the Sterling Cross luxury jewelry company. Threats were issued, violent ones, to make Wolfe Capital pull out, and I just know Sebastian's been burning for payback ever since. He's invited Nero to his card games before, wanting a chance to best him, but Nero never took the bait.

Miles wasn't so lucky.

A waiter passes with a tray of champagne, and I grab a glass and take a gulp. I'm keeping my wits sharp tonight, but I need something to help take the edge off: that sting of grief that threatens to bubble to the surface every time I think of him.

Miles Romero. The only man I've ever loved. A good man, too, despite the blood and violence of the world we grew up in. He had a sweetness to him, a gentle, trusting side. He used to scold me for being so jaded. He said everyone had some good in them, if you looked hard enough.

Is that what he thought about Sebastian Wolfe, I wonder? Did he walk into a room like this one, thinking he could trust the men trading hundred-thousand-dollar gambling tokens like candy? That a man like Sebastian would play by the rules?

He should have known; the devil always wins.

And that's what I'm counting on tonight.

"Smile, sweetheart," Nero says loudly, pulling me back to our audience. He gives me a cocky smirk. "You're here to look pretty, not scowl all night."

"I'm sorry." I murmur, forcing a nervous smile. Nero smirks wider. He knows that any other time, an instruction like that would earn him a slap. But we want to make it clear to the crowd, I have no say here. I'm just arm candy. A pretty bauble.

Ready to be traded.

"Well, look who we have here." Sebastian Wolfe finally saunters to the table, taking his seat. "Nero Barretti," he smirks, looking like it was a victory just having us here. "You finally decided to join us."

Nero shrugs. "I was in the neighborhood, figured I'd check out your little game."

7

"*Little...*" Sebastian echoes. He's still smiling, but I can see the resentment in his eyes—burning almost as hot at the vengeance inside me. "You won't have any problem meeting the buy-in, then?"

"Nah." Nero pulls a roll of cash from his pocket and tosses it on the card table. "Two hundred Gs, right?"

"For starters." Sebastian seems amused. "But I should warn you, it won't last long."

"I can handle my business." Nero glares. He gives me the cash. "Hold it, babe."

I tuck it into my purse, feeling Sebastian's eyes on me. He doesn't say anything though, just turns to the rest of the players and raises his glass. "Let the games begin."

The dealer shuffles, and then it's on. Hand after hand, the stakes getting higher with every game. Nero starts strong, the way we planned, but once there are just a few hardcore gamblers left at the table, he starts to slip: Betting wildly, drinking hard and cursing with every loss, growing more reckless as the night continues and his stack of chips disappears until finally, a hand comes around when everybody else has folded, and it's just him and Sebastian left in the game.

I blink to attention, my pulse suddenly racing. This is it, the moment I've been waiting for. My shot.

I lean forwards, on edge as Nero glances at his cards. "Raise," he demands.

Sebastian quirks an eyebrow. "I believe your bank is empty."

"Then fill it up," Nero growls, stripping off his watch and tossing it in. "There, that's worth a hundred grand, easy."

Sebastian shrugs. "Suit yourself. I see your hundred... and I raise another two."

There's a buzz of excitement in the room. There must be a million bucks already on the table. But Nero is out of chips.

Sebastian's smile grows wider. "Ready to call it a night?" he asks smugly.

"Fuck no," Nero says, gulping scotch. "I'll see your two and raise another two. I'm good for it."

Sebastian's lip curls. "We don't accept IOUs here."

Nero shoves back from the table so hard the glasses rattle. "Are you questioning my word?"

Sebastian stares back evenly, not intimidated at all. "I'm questioning your funds. And if you don't have them, it's time to fold."

Nero scowls. "It's OK," I reach out to soothe him, but he slaps my hand away.

"What else?" he demands, looking to Sebastian. "What else will you take?"

"That depends, Mr. Barretti," Sebastian says, lounging there with a dangerous smile on his face. "What else do you have to offer?"

Nero look around, as if he's thinking fast. Then his gaze lands on me.

"Her."

A gasp ripples through the crowd, but Sebastian's face is unreadable. His gaze drifts over me, impassive. "For how much?" he asks, casually, like he's talking about another designer watch, and not a living, breathing woman.

"A million," Nero says immediately.

I pretend to gasp. "What are you doing?" I protest, like I haven't planned every moment of this. Dreamed about it. Obsessed over it, late into the night.

"Shut the fuck up," Nero growls at me.

"No!" My voice rises in distress. "You can't do this!" I look around the room, at all the faces staring at me in scandalized excitement. At Sebastian Wolfe's icy gaze.

And then I burst into tears and rush from the room.

9

Nero follows me, heading to the balcony that juts out over the cliffs. I pace, anxious, everything riding on these next few minutes.

"Looks like he's buying it," Nero murmurs quietly.

I give the smallest of nods. We're close, I can tell, but Sebastian Wolfe is no fool. He hasn't built a vast fortune with trust and optimism. If I'm going to close this deal, my performance needs to be flawless—even if nobody is around to see. *Yet.*

"How could you?" I cry, whirling on Nero. "I'm not your property to be auctioned off to the highest bidder!"

"You're wrong about that." Nero replies loudly.

"No." I shake my head furiously. "I won't go with him. You can't make me!"

"Can't I?"

Nero suddenly lunges at me, grabbing me by the throat and leaning me back over the balcony railings. "You'll do whatever the fuck I say," he growls threateningly, and I gasp in surprise. The waves are crashing against the rocks below me, and if I didn't know Nero better—if I hadn't planned this whole night— the look in his eyes would chill me to the core.

I'm still bent back, his fingers closed around my neck, when somebody clears their throat.

"I hate to interrupt," Sebastian's voice comes from the doorway. "But the game waits for no man."

Nero releases his grip, and I gulp for air, stumbling upright. "Sure, let's play," he says quickly, acting jittery, like a man betting too much on a losing hand. "Come on, doll."

He grabs my arm roughly, dragging me towards the door. I struggle, turning my gaze to Seb, pleading. "Please..." I murmur pitifully. "Please don't do this."

Sebastian pauses, looking from Nero to me and back again.

My heart skips a beat. If he was a good man, then this is where he would intervene. Take me away from this violent mafia king, reassure me that everything will be OK. That I'm safe. That he would never trade my body over a hand of cards.

But I already know, Sebastian Wolfe is no good man. He's a monster. The reason Miles took his own life.

And sure enough, his gaze is cold, unmoved by my pleas. "Will she be a problem?" he asks Nero, like I'm not even standing here.

Like I'm nothing but currency to him.

"She'll behave." Nero scowls. "If she knows what's good for her."

"Either way..." Sebastian's lips curl in a cruel smile. "I'll have fun breaking her in."

I can't help the shudder of revulsion that rolls through me at his words. Sebastian sees, but his smile just spreads wider.

"We have a game to finish."

Nero yanks me back inside, to where everyone is still waiting at the card table. I look around the room at the curious, expectant faces, and swallow my disgust. They don't know I've orchestrated every moment of this; they're just watching like it's entertainment. Like my virtue is just another young, expensive bauble to be traded away in a game between billionaires.

I sink back into my seat. A glass of champagne appears at my side, and I gulp it quickly, nervous all over again.

This is it.

Nero glances at his cards again, and nods to the dealer. "Hit me."

"Wait." Sebastian's voice makes the dealer freeze. "I've changed my mind."

No!

I gape at him in panic. Sebastian turns and meets my gaze, giving me a slow, assessing stare. "You offered one night with her, against a million-dollar stake," he says, not looking away. "I want a month."

A month?

It takes everything I have to seem devastated, but inside, I'm conflicted between victory and suspicion. This is exactly what I wanted. The chance to get close to him, to infiltrate his life. I was expecting to have to charm and seduce him to get inside his fortress, but instead, he offers that access up on a platter?

I don't understand it. What is he planning?

"A month with the girl," Sebastian continues, "and I'll stake you ten million."

A hum of shock ripples around the room, but Nero doesn't even hesitate. "Done," he says with a growl.

He takes the card from the dealer, and smirks.

"Call."

Everyone leans closer as Nero turns his cards, and even I'm on the edge of my seat. He's good enough to make losing look easy, but if Sebastian suspects even for a second that Nero's thrown the game...

"Full house," Nero says with a cocky smile.

I exhale.

It's a good hand. Maybe even too good. I gulp, wondering if anything can beat it. If Nero's fucked this up on purpose, and all my careful midnight plans will be for nothing.

But then I see it: the unmistakable flash of victory in Sebastian's gaze. He takes his time revealing his cards, but I already know the result.

Emotion crashes through me. Victory, and fear, and regret, all at once. But it's too late to change my mind now. The deal has been struck.

"Royal flush," he announces, and the crowd goes wild. Celebrating this grotesque victory—and everything it means. Cheering my sacrifice.

It sickens me, but isn't that a good thing? Just another reminder of what I'm up against.

Another flame to the fire of my simmering rage.

As the other players swarm Sebastian with congratulations, Nero approaches me, looking guilty as fuck. "I'm sorry," he says in a low voice, and I know it's true. He tried to talk me out of this. Not because he doesn't believe in justice, but because his kind comes at the end of a .45. He would happily put a bullet in Sebastian's head for what he's done, but that isn't good enough for me.

I want him broken. Ruined. Begging for the release of death.

"Just go," I tell Nero, clenching my jaw. I need to appear angry with him, but the truth is, I need him gone. He's the only person in this room who knows who I truly am under the dress and the diamonds. Before everything changed. I can't have him looking at me like that, like I'm still that girl. If I'm going to do this, I need to be untouchable.

Vengeance made flesh.

Nero nods, understanding. "Good luck," he whispers softly, and then he's gone, back to his new bride, and her redeeming love, and a world that keeps spinning, even without Miles in it.

But I'm not so lucky. Miles was everything to me, the only good thing in all the darkness.

Which means there's nobody coming to drag me back up to the light.

I drift back out onto the balcony, draining my glass of champagne. I have a headache, and feel kind of nauseous, but maybe that's just the jet lag. I take a deep breath of salty ocean air, and wonder what's to come. For all my planning, I have no idea what happens next. I set a trap for Sebastian Wolfe, using my body as bait, but now that he's walked into it...?

Anything could happen.

The ocean is dark now, an inky mass crashing against the glittering shoreline. The breeze has cooled, and I shiver, not even realizing I've been joined out here until a jacket is placed around my shoulders.

I startle.

"Easy there." It's Sebastian, regarding me with that cool amusement in his eyes. He towers over me even in my heels, and I feel off-balance, too small and delicate against his lean, muscular frame. "You're awfully skittish."

"Do you blame me?" I shoot back. It's a relief that I don't have to mask my loathing anymore. Any woman in her right mind would be furious about the stunt the guys just pulled. "I thought Barretti was scum, but you?"

"What about me?"

Sebastian fixes me with a cool, predatory gaze, and I shiver.

"I want to leave," I say, my voice quavering. I frown. I wasn't even trying to make it shake, but suddenly, I'm feeling unsteady.

"Certainly." Sebastian says. "Where shall we go?"

I shake my head, holding on to the balcony railing now for balance. "I didn't mean with you..." I say, trying to think straight.

What's happening? My head is spinning, but I've only had a couple of glasses of champagne, and I've been drinking guys under the table for years.

"You know the deal," Sebastian says, sounding bored. "You're mine, for the month."

"I didn't agree to that." I protest feebly.

"But Barretti did. So if you're thinking about slipping out after your boyfriend, don't." Sebastian adds coolly. "I always collect my debts."

My vision blurs, and my legs suddenly give way. I have the terrible sensation of free fall. It seems to last forever, like my rage has become gravity, pulling me under. I dimly register Sebastian's arms catching me before I hit the ground, but instead of safety at his embrace, I only feel an icy fear spread through my veins.

None of this is turning out the way I planned. But now there's no going back.

Not until Sebastian Wolfe is dead in the ground—or wishes he was.

Chapter 3

Avery

I *fucked up.*
I got in too deep with Sebastian's card game, I tried covering from the accounts, I thought I could win it back again, but I failed.
I let you down.
I'm sorry
- M

I come back into consciousness with a throbbing pain in my head, and the words from Miles' suicide note echoing in my mind. I groan as I open my eyes, finding myself in a strange room, wearing a fluffy of bathrobe. My heart races as I sit up, the pain in my head increasing.

What the hell happened?

I'm in a gorgeous bedroom with white stucco walls and sunlight streaming between the parted curtains. The only furniture is a single antique dresser and the huge king-sized bed. It's a huge four-poster bed with the softest mattress I've ever been on and the kind of linens that would put a hotel to shame.

I have no idea where I am or how I got here.

Fear is thick in my blood as I search my memory of last night, but there's a blank space in my mind. I start to get out of the bed, my bare feet meeting cool wood on the floors. Then I see the white dress from last night laid carefully over the back of a chair.

Suddenly, it all comes back to me.

The poker game. Nero's bet. My plan to destroy Sebastian Wolfe.

He took the bait.

But what happened next? I wonder, panicking. Why is my memory blank? And who undressed me last night? I stand and my head swims like a bad hangover, but I didn't drink anything. Only that one glass of champagne—

I freeze. Did Sebastian drug me?

The thought sends a new chill through me. I didn't see that coming. I can't help wondering if I'm in over my head here.

Panic is creeping over me, but I remind myself of exactly who I'm dealing with and why I decided to do this. I knew Sebastian was dangerous going into this crazy plan. It's why Nero was so reluctant to go along with it. But it doesn't matter. I'm on a mission, playing a part.

I'm doing this in memory of a man I loved.

Steeling my nerves, I walk over to the window and pull back the curtains. My breath leaves me as I look out at the endless ocean. The cloudless sky is a brilliant blue and the waves are rolling in on the golden sand.

And I don't see any other buildings around.

I shiver. This isn't St. Tropez. There, you can't move for fancy boutiques and stylish hotels, especially on the shoreline.

So where the hell am I?

I look to the left and right as much as I can. I see a rocky cliff in one direction and palm trees in the other, and no land in sight. Am I on some kind of island?

Just how long have I been knocked out?

I try to pull myself together, but questions are whirling in my mind. I thought I had the upper hand, that I'd planned for everything, but clearly, Sebastian is one step ahead of me.

So now I have to wonder...

Does he know who I really am?

Glancing down, I see a stone terrace directly beneath me. As I watch, Sebastian steps into view, his cell phone pressed to his ear. He's dressed down, for him, in linen pants and a white button-down shirt, and he paces, talking.

He glances up at the window, and I duck back before he can see me.

Why are you hiding, Avery? I ask myself. *You don't cower from a fight. Not with anyone.*

It's time to go get some answers from the man.

I throw open the bedroom doors, and stride out, still barefoot in the robe. The house is just as big and impressive as I would have imagined: a long hallway leading past many other rooms to a grand staircase. On the ground floor, there's a dining room that could easily fit a two-dozen people at the long table and a vast living room, filled with chic designer furniture. One entire wall is glass, pulled back to lead seamlessly to the terrace, so I gather my wits and every last ounce of courage, and steam outside.

Anger is good. Any innocent young woman would be scared and confused right now.

Sebastian has finished his call, and is lounging at a table, set for breakfast.

My resentment surges to the surface at the sight of him

relaxed in his chair, looking out at the water. It's like he doesn't have a care in the world.

Like he didn't kidnap a woman last night.

"Where the hell are we?" I demand.

He glances up as I stalk over. "Good morning," he says evenly, his dark hair still wet from the shower, falling rumpled just over his cut-glass blue eyes. "Did you sleep well?"

"Fine, thanks to whatever it is you drugged me with! And you didn't answer my question, where are we?"

He gives a shrug. "A small island in the Balearics," he replies, looking amused. "I use it for occasional getaways. The privacy suits me. No unwanted interruptions. Do you like it?"

I recoil at his smug, even temper. "I want to leave. Now."

"Are you forgetting that you're my prize?" Sebastian asks, slowly getting to his feet. I'm reminded how much he towers over me, his taut frame sauntering closer, powerful as a panther ready to strike. Even dressed down, he's still sharp and crisp, everything about him screaming control and luxury.

I take a small step back.

"Or are you planning to renege on the deal?" he asks, searching my face. "Keep in mind, Nero will owe me ten million if you do. And I'm guessing he isn't a man you want to cross. We have that much in common, at least."

I want to scream at him, to tell him just how much of a bastard he is, but I remember the innocent and shy role I'm supposed to be playing.

I drop my eyes and hug my arms around myself, trying to appear modest. I even tug the robe tighter, as if I'm self-conscious about the fact I'm nearly naked beneath it.

Think, Avery.

I bite my lip as I consider how to respond. It's not difficult to appear nervous since I am. My plan has already gone way off-script with this whole 'kidnapping' curveball. Clearly, we're alone out here, and I need to figure out what he's planning.

"There's no need to contact Nero," I say, putting just the right amount of anxiety in my voice to sell my fear of him. "But... I don't know what you want from me."

Sebastian's eyes drift over my body. "Oh, I'm sure you can imagine, a pretty little thing like you?"

I shiver, thrown by the blatant sexuality in his gaze.

"I want to make sure you understand... I'm not going to..." I wish there was a way to make myself blush, but I'm not really the demure princess I'm pretending to be and there are some things that can't be faked. I just clear my throat and drop my eyes, as if I'm deeply embarrassed. "You won my presence, my company. Nothing more."

Sebastian looks amused. "Are you sure about that?"

I look up sharply. "Yes. Unless you're the kind of man who would force a woman..."

Right away, Sebastian gives me an icy stare. "I've never had to *force* a woman to do anything. On the contrary," he adds, the glare smoothing to a seductive smirk. "I like my women moaning for more."

His voice drops, and he takes another step closer. "Is that how you'll be, my sweet?" he reaches out and runs his fingertips down my cheek. "I bet you'll look so pretty on your knees, begging for my cock."

I lurch back as if I've been burned, blushing furiously for real this time. "N-no, I won't." I blurt, my heart racing from the illicit image he just conjured. What is happening? My cheek tingles where he touched it, as if his fingers left a mark.

Sebastian just smiles, dark and imposing. "We'll see. I think you'll be surprised at what you'll be asking by the end of the month. What those pretty lips will do." He gives a chuckle, and I feel a shudder roll through me.

But not the revulsion I would expect for a man like this. It's something else.

Something far more dangerous.

As I'm reeling, flustered, Sebastian's phone buzzes on the table. He turns away from me, like I'm not even there anymore. "I have business to attend to," he says, not looking up from the screen. "Make yourself at home," he adds. "The staff is at your disposal."

Sebastian leaves without another word, and a moment later, a butler emerges with a coffee press. "Miss?" he asks politely, with a French accent. "Would you like me to fix you anything to eat? Omelet? Crepes? Un petit croissant?"

My stomach rumbles on command, reminding me that it's been a day, at least, since I've managed to eat anything. "All of them, please," I decide, taking a seat and catching my breath. Now Sebastian is out of sight, my tension eases—just a little. This is a temporary respite, I know, but I'm going to take advantage of it. If I'm trapped on this island with a private chef, the least I can do is fuel myself for the fight ahead.

And boy, does that coffee smell good.

* * *

I finish breakfast, then return to my room, guessing Sebastian—or his staff—will have provided me with clothing, since my luggage is still somewhere in the South of France.

I'm right. I quickly explore the room and find that there are clothes in the dresser and closet. They're all my size and styled to match the persona I've been performing: all preppy, innocent sundresses and chic little designer outfits. In the huge marble bathroom, there are luxurious toiletries, beauty products, every kind of appliance and accessory... Someone has stocked the place perfectly for a female guest.

Maybe this is where he brings all his gambling trophies.

I shower and pick out a simple pink sundress from the closet. There's a designer tag, and the cost would pay my rent for a month back in the city, but I pull it on with fresh lingerie, blow-drying my hair and adding makeup, too. It's a change not reaching for the heavy eyeliner, or badass lipstick stain, but I guess I was dressing to send a message back in New York, too. *Don't fuck with me.*

What message should I be sending now, I wonder. Seduce me? Covet me?

Love me?

Once I'm dressed, I feel better. More like an actress, playing a role. Because I am one. And I can't risk breaking character for a moment, not with Sebastian so close.

And my plan for revenge underway.

There's still no sign of him when I go back downstairs, so I spend the day exploring my surroundings. I need to get my head wrapped around where I am and what's to come. The island is gorgeous, with sand and ocean everywhere I look. I take a long walk on the beach, breathing in the salty air. I try to calm myself and focus, but it's impossible. This place is a paradise, but I feel like I'm in hell.

And I'm stuck with the devil.

After idly roaming as far as I dare, I return to the house, for some real exploring. After all, everything I'm doing is in order to get close to Sebastian.

To discover his secrets. His weaknesses.

And use them against him.

So, I tentatively wander the gleaming, minimal rooms. It's vast and airy—and has exactly zero personal touches. No photographs, no mementos—at least—not on display in the main rooms. Maybe they're shut away somewhere, or maybe a ruthless business titan like Sebastian doesn't have a soft spot for personal items. I come across the butler reading a newspaper in the kitchens, and a woman dusting the sleek furniture, but otherwise, no one else is present.

I'm alone here with him.

Finally, I discover a music room, towards the back of the house. There's a couch, record player, and a grand piano, sitting in the corner. Untouched.

It's been a long time since I played. There's not much use for classical piano in the mafia underworld, but I find myself drifting over and taking a seat on the polished bench. It's a gorgeous instrument, and I can't resist the urge to lift the fall-board and place my fingers on the keys. It's perfectly tuned. I don't even have to think about what I want to play. A few seconds of tinkering around to warm up, and I'm ready.

The first notes of "Let It Be" by The Beatles have an immediate calming effect on me. The melody is soothing, a memory of a happier time. I close my eyes, letting myself get lost in the music. I start to sing along, lyrics that I didn't even realize I remembered flowing out me, and I pour my heart into it.

For just a few moments, I forget about the seriousness of my situation and let my grief fall to the back of my mind. It's a relief, even though I know it won't last.

When the song ends, I let out a breath of longing. For the happier time, when I would play more often. When I was innocent about the world, and all the dark deeds that happened in it.

The sound of applause snaps me out of my reverie. I open my eyes, and startle at the sight of Sebastian in the doorway, watching me. "Bravo," he says, and I can't tell if his tone is sarcastic.

It must be.

I'm mortified. I didn't expect him to catch me singing. It's something I only do in private. I feel exposed. Even the people closest to me haven't heard my voice like this.

"I'm sorry," I blurt, jolting up from the stool. "I just found it, and—"

Sebastian holds up a hand, silencing me.

"No need to apologize. Please, a fine instrument deserves to be played, don't you think?"

I flush at the double meaning.

Sebastian crosses the room and takes a seat on the small bench beside me. There's barely room for the both of us, and his thigh is pressed against mine, hot.

"You... Play?" I blurt, unnerved by his sudden presence beside me.

I can smell him. The low, spicy notes of his aftershave drift through the air between us, and when he places his hands on the keys, his arm presses against mine.

"A little," Sebastian replies.

His fingers, long and nimble, go to the keys, and he starts to play another song I recognize. "Desperado" by The Eagles was a favorite of my father's. He's the one that taught me to play, so I learned all the older songs he loved.

I feel a surge of nostalgia.

After a moment, I can't resist joining him, playing the piano in a kind of duet. I don't sing again, but Sebastian doesn't seem to mind, he hums along beside me, picking out the notes, giving a rueful chuckle when he fumbles a key, until finally, the song ends.

The corners of his mouth quirk up in a ghost of a smile. "Aren't you full of surprises?" he says, looking at me.

Too close.

"I could say the same about you," I manage to reply. His closeness is unnerving to me. I can see the faint shadow of stubble on his strong jaw, and the crease of lines around his eyes that only add to his sense of authority.

"You have no idea." Sebastian stands. "Now, go get dressed for dinner."

"Dinner?"

"Yes. It's a big night. I want you to look your best, Sparrow."

I feel an uncomfortable jolt at his pet name, but I swallow back my reaction.

Play your part.

"Fine," I say obediently, getting to my feet. "Whatever you want."

Sebastian smirks at that, and I leave the room before he can see the anger burning in my eyes.

The longer he thinks that's how this is going to go, the sooner he'll show his cards.

Chapter 4

Avery

I take a long, luxurious bubble bath in the massive tub, then dress for dinner. I'm full of nerves, wondering what Sebastian has planned.

He wants to seduce me, that much is clear—from his lingering looks and suggestive words. And sure, I knew that, coming into this mission. My sexuality is a weapon, and I'm prepared to use it however I need to. But still, I don't want to just be a one-night conquest that he discards in the morning. I need more than that, if my plan is going to work.

So how am I going to manage this, walking the line to keep him interested, but still giving him nothing in return?

It seems impossible. I'm not experienced in seduction, like the women I see in the Barretti world. They come and go from the club where I bartend: Brassy, confident women who are totally in control of their sexuality, hooking up with the guys, and walking away with a smile on their faces. Sure, I know enough to fake the same confidence, but underneath all that?

I have no idea what I'm doing with men.

I sigh, pulling on the white silk lingerie that's waiting in a drawer. I pick out another demure outfit, this one a pale blue dress with straps that tie like ribbons on my shoulders. The neckline is high, and the skirt floats down past my knees. I look like a princess, a debutante virgin who has spent her life telling horny men 'No thank you'.

The truth is, that virgin part is no lie.

I'm twenty-one-years-old, and I've never been with a man. Never even had him touch me the way I touch myself at night, when I close my eyes and sink into the velvet rush of fantasy and my own fast fingers. And sure, I've had my chances. Guys ask me out all the time. Hell, with the number of Barretti men hanging around, I've been fighting them off since I turned fifteen and filled out my sports bras.

But I waited. For Miles.

He was the only one I loved, the only one I wanted to share that part of myself with. I knew, one day, all the mafia chaos would be behind us, and we would be together.

But now that day will never come.

I feel a sting of anger. Because that's another thing Sebastian took from me, when he drove Miles to take his own life. The future we could have shared together.

All my waiting has been in vain.

I cross to my purse, the small, glittered clutch from last night was the only thing Sebastian brought here with me. I'm sure he would have searched it, but I was expecting that.

I open it, and carefully ease the lining away from the seam, to find the hidden pocket. Inside, is a locket. With Miles' photo inside. It's from an old photo-strip, we took it at Coney Island, in one of the old-fashioned booths, skipping out of the city for the day to ride the roller-coasters and eat salt-water taffy on the shore.

It was a perfect day. I look at his goofy, smiling face, and feel my resolve strengthen.

27

Whatever it takes, it'll be worth it to avenge his death.

I finish dressing and go downstairs. The dining room is dark and empty, but I can see lights and some staff outside, so I follow them to where a beautiful candlelit table has been set up by the edge of the cliffs. There are fresh flowers, linen table-cloth, silver cutlery... With the moon overhead on a clear night, and the dark waves crashing below, it looks like something out of a romance scene.

Too bad the effect leaves me cold.

"What do you think?" Sebastian's voice makes me turn. He's approaching, dressed in a suit, with his shirt open at the collar. I know a hundred—if not a thousand—women would be swooning over a handsome man like this, staging a romantic dinner, but I can't bring myself to pretend I'm one of them.

"It looks lovely," I say evenly, and take a seat. "Do you treat all your gambling wins like this?"

Sebastian chuckles. "Only the most beautiful," he says, nodding for the staff to leave. He picks up a bottle. "Champagne?"

"Fine." I shrug. Then I remember, I can't be surly or offended for too long. Sebastian might lose interest and figure I'm too much of a downer. "Thank you," I add, giving him a shy smile.

He pulls out my chair for me, then pours us both a glass. "Cheers," he says, raising his in a toast to me.

"What are we drinking to?" I ask.

"To... unexpected new acquaintances." Sebastian is still watching me, like he's gauging my mood.

I give a wry smile. "Unexpected is right," I say, clinking my glass to his and taking a sip. "When I left America, I definitely didn't think I'd wind up here. With you."

Sebastian seems to relax a little. The server brings our first course, some kind of beef tartare. I poke it, dubious.

"Here, you need to mix it in with the egg yolk, and lemon. It's delicious," he reassures me, and reaches over to prepare the dish for me.

"Thank you," I say. "I'm not exactly used to fancy food, or fine dining."

"No?" Sebastian seems surprised. "I would have thought... But never mind. How did you find yourself with Nero?"

I look down. "Much the same way I found myself with you," I say quietly. "My pops used to have a saying, 'Out of the frying pan, into the fire.' That's kind of what the past few weeks have been like for me."

I glance up. Sure enough, Sebastian is fixed on me, curious. "Tell me more."

I've been over my fake backstory a dozen times, and it almost feels natural as I explain.

"I grew up with my dad, upstate. We had a small farm, and I guess things got rough, because it turns out, he was in debt to the Barrettis. I didn't know, not until after he passed, and Nero showed up to take the farm. He saw me, and, well... He let me stay with an aunt of mine, the past few years, until I turned twenty-one. And then... Then he came to collect."

I look down again, playing the innocent.

"And did he?" Sebastian asks, taking a sip of champagne.

"What?"

"Collect."

My eyes fly up at the question. "I... Don't know what you mean."

"I think you do." Sebastian's lips curl in a knowing smile.

I flush, for real this time. There's something about the candlelight and champagne. I feel exposed. Like Sebastian's blunt questions are stripping me bare, right in front of him.

I shake my head. "I... I was supposed to be his reward. For beating you, at the poker game," I say.

And I know my demure answer is the right one, because Sebastian's smile grows.

Of course it does. Now, I'm not just Nero's stolen plaything, but the prize even his rival hasn't enjoyed yet.

"Interesting," is all he says, and then changes the subject. "Ah, the next course. Jacques makes an incredible lobster; you have to taste it to believe."

I exhale, relieved.

"What about you?" I ask, when we're alone again. "What's your story?"

I fix him with a curious smile, and this time, I'm not faking. I want to know everything I can about this man. And I may not know much about guys, but I do know they love talking about themselves, and will go on and on at the smallest prompt.

But not Sebastian. He gives a small shrug. "Nothing to tell."

"Oh, come on," I prompt him. "You don't get to have a place like this, or play ten-million-dollar poker hands, without an interesting journey. You have some kind of financial company, right?"

He nods. "Wolfe Capital. A hedge fund."

"And that means...?" I give a little giggle.

"We buy out companies. Restructure, reinvest. Sell for a profit," Sebastian replies evenly.

I remember that this is how his rivalry with Nero started. Sebastian tried to launch a hostile takeover of Sterling Cross, a luxury jewelry company Nero was involved in. Nero made him back off, and I'm guessing it was not through normal legal channels. Sebastian has been trying to get back at him ever since, and getting Miles caught up in his poker game was part of it.

We're all just pawns to him.

"I guess you're pretty good at it then, judging by all of this." I manage to coo, swallowing back my resentment with another swig of champagne.

"I like to win." Sebastian says, giving me a look. "At any cost."

"I kind of guessed. You know, from the poker game," I add.

"It's a fun pastime." Sebastian sits back, relaxing. "Helps me blow off steam."

"I don't know, it seems kind of stressful to me." I give another self-conscious giggle. "I mean, how can you relax with so much on the line?"

"I didn't say anything about relaxing," Sebastian replies, looking amused. "I enjoy the high stakes, taking a risk."

"And making unexpected new acquaintances," I quip.

He smiles. "That too."

He's good at ducking questions, but that's OK. I have time. A whole month, if he really meant what he told Nero at the game.

"So did you always want to start your own company?" I ask.

Sebastian flinches. It's the smallest movement, a tightening of his jaw, but I see it.

I see everything.

"My father started Wolfe Capital," he replies shortly. "He built it from nothing."

I knew that, but I didn't know what his reaction would be. *Interesting.*

"Oh, that must have been nice." I beam. "A family business. Are you two close?"

"We were." Another clipped answer. "He died, when I was seventeen."

"I'm so sorry!" I exclaim, pressing a hand to my chest. "That must have been awful. I miss my papa too," I add. "Every day."

Sebastian meets my eyes, and I wonder if I catch a glimpse of understanding there. Then the shutters slam down again, and he gives a shrug.

"It was a long time ago. Ancient history."

"And now you're continuing his legacy," I add, with another encouraging smile. "I'm sure he would be very proud of you, to see everything you've achieved."

Sebastian gives a sharp, bitter-sounding laugh. "No, he wouldn't."

He tosses back the rest of his champagne and gets to his feet. "Dance with me," he commands, holding out his hand.

I blink, startled. "I... But there isn't any music."

Sebastian takes out his phone and taps a few times. Music suddenly plays all around us from hidden speakers, embedded in the stone.

"Dance with me," he repeats, stone-faced, and I know there's no refusing him.

I get to my feet, and slowly walk over to join him. He takes one of my hands in his, and places his other on the small of my back, drawing me closer like the old-fashioned musicals I used to watch on TV.

I inhale a shaky breath. This is the closest I've ever been to him, our bodies touching, with my eyes just level with his chest. He moves quietly, with surprising grace. Or maybe I shouldn't be surprised. Sebastian Wolfe never does anything badly.

"You're tense," he remarks in a low voice, and his breath whispers, hot against my forehead.

"Can you blame me?" I shoot back without thinking, then curse myself. I'm supposed to be flustered and innocent, not full of rage for the man.

But Sebastian just chuckles. "Relax," he says, and suddenly spins me out, then back into his arms. This time, I stumble into them, even closer than before. I can feel his chest pressed against me, the low pump of his heart. The vein in his neck beating softly, inches away.

I could lunge for a steak knife, and slash his throat wide open, right here. Drive it between his ribs and into his heart. I know the place--

"What are you thinking?" Sebastian's voice breaks my blood-soaked fantasies.

"Nothing," I blurt. "Just... this is nice."

Nice.

Only a fool would believe I could go from spitting mad to swooning in the space of an hour, but maybe Sebastian is just a man, because he settles his arms around me, bringing one to trace slow circles on the bare nape of my neck.

His touch shivers through me.

I want to recoil, but I force myself not to move. I just stay there, swaying in the iron circle of his embrace, as his fingertips brush over my shoulders... my neck... the tops of my arms....

My skin prickles. My whole body tightens.

I pull away. "What do you want from me—really?" I blurt, my cheeks flushing. "You brought me here; I've agreed to stay the month. At least be honest with me."

Sebastian looks down at me, his face shadowed in the moonlight. "I told you, I like to win," he replies cryptically. "I'm bored, I thought you'd be a diverting amusement, but now..."

"Now?" I echo with a gulp.

"Now, I suspect you're more interesting than you seem." Sebastian's eyes burn into me.

I give a nervous laugh. "I'm really not," I say quickly.

"On the contrary, Miss Carmichael," Sebastian tilts his head, assessing. "I read people rather well. It's what makes me unbeatable at poker. And you? You have yet to show your hand."

"What makes you think I'll show it to you?" I ask, arching an eyebrow.

Sebastian steps back, smiling. "And there it is," he says, sounding satisfied. "The kitten has some claws."

"I'm not a kitten," I roll my eyes.

"No, you're the Little Sparrow," Sebastian agrees.

I sigh. Clearly, the man isn't in the mood to answer any questions tonight, and I'm not about to stick around to have him turn them around on me. I finish my champagne and give him a smile. "It's too late for all these metaphors, and I've had a long day. You know, with the kidnapping, and all."

Sebastian chuckles again, amused. "Goodnight, Sparrow."

"Can you please not call me that?" I ask.

"That depends," Sebastian smirks. "Do I get a goodnight kiss?"

I pause. He's looking at me, like there's no way he expects me to rise to the challenge.

I narrow my eyes. "Fine."

I lean up on my tiptoes and press my lips quickly to his cheek. "There," I say, beginning to pull away. "Goodnight."

"Not good enough." Sebastian growls, catching my wrist. "Try again."

I stare up at him, caught. There's a look in his eyes I've never seen before—and definitely not directed at me. It's hot, possessive. *Wanting.*

"I..." I'm stuttering my reply when Sebastian reaches out, cups my face between both hands, and kisses me.

For real. On the mouth, this time.

It's soft. Barely even a whisper. I'm not expecting it—the kiss, or his gentleness. I was braced for something cruel and dominant, not this slow, teasing caress of his mouth on mine.

Oh.

I sway against him in surprise, my lips parting of their own accord.

Sebastian eases them wider, and slowly strokes his tongue into my mouth.

The kiss deepens, Sebastian bringing me closer, his tongue making a soft, thorough exploration of my willing mouth. He makes a low groan of approval, and an answering shudder rolls through me, something hot and sweet that seems to seep through my bloodstream, pooling between my thighs like molasses.

Like poison.

I snatch away, shaken to my now-aching core. "I... Umm..." I blurt, wild-eyed. "Sleep. I need it. Goodnight!"

I turn and flee for the house. Sebastian doesn't stop me, but he doesn't have to. His touch is still echoing through my body, reminding me with every step just how dangerous the man is.

And how much more ruthless I need to be to take him down.

Chapter 5

Avery

I can't sleep.

Even with the drapes drawn, and the most comfortable bed in the world cradling me in softness, my mind is too busy, and my body is too wired to just drift off to sleep.

Too wired, and... *Turned on.*

Guilt and shame ricochet through me, and I bury my face in the pillows in despair.

How could I be turned on by a kiss with that monster?

I don't understand it. Nothing about Sebastian Wolfe is attractive to me. Sure, I can see his objective appeal, how other women might bat their eyelashes and gossip over his well-cut suits and classically handsome features, but those things leave me cold. I know who he is underneath it all.

A heartless man. The enemy I've sworn to destroy.

So why does my body still tighten with the memory of his slow, seductive touch?

Why do my lips burn from his unexpected kiss?

I sit up, flushed and breathless. *It's not real*, I vow, getting up to pace in the dark room. This is a symptom of my inexperience, that's all. If I'd kissed more men, or had more sexual adventures in my life, then none of this would even register. I would be cold as marble. Indifferent.

Not itching with a restless ache inside, craving... Something.

Something from him.

No.

I take a deep breath, and then another. I need to get myself under control. If I get thrown for a loop like this on our very first night together, how am I supposed to stay committed to my mission?

My body is an instrument, like that polished Steinway downstairs. I repeat the words over to myself in the hush of the darkness. Sebastian can touch it, sure, play whatever melody he thinks he wants to hear, but whatever happens, he can't touch *me*.

Only I can choose who sees the real me. Who I share that with.

The way I shared my heart with Miles.

Slowly, my heart rate slows, but I know that I'm never going to sleep when I'm still wound this tightly. Pulling on a silky robe, I ease the bedroom door open and check around.

The hallway is dark. It's past midnight now, and the house is silent.

I creep out, barefoot, and slowly pad downstairs. I already looked around, but I'm in search of something more now. This whole place looks like something out of a magazine, but nobody can live in a blank canvas like this, not without losing their mind.

Unless he's a sociopath. Which, the jury's still out on that.

I figure Sebastian must have some personal things, somewhere. Some insight that will help me figure him out. So, I search every room again, looking in drawers and cabinets, and checking every locked door. Even if this is only a vacation island, it's still his place, after all.

Ha. I have to stifle a hollow laugh at that. Who the hell has a vacation *island?*

I grew up spending a week on the Jersey shore with my parents every summer, if I was lucky. But usually, my dad had pressing Barretti business—the kind we never asked about, the kind he came home from with bruises—so I spent the summers sweltering in the city, eating ice-pops, and daring Miles to bust open a sprinkler in the park.

I feel an ache of sadness at the memory. Of more innocent times, when we still had no real idea what life had in store for the both of us.

Or death.

Bingo. I'm not even paying attention, when a random door-knob turns, and I step into a room I must have missed on my first look around. It's a long, sleek gallery space, filled with modern art and sculpture. Even I can recognize some of the pieces hanging on the pristine white walls. Rothko. Warhol. Banksy.

I gape. The art in here must be worth a fortune. And not a small one, either. These paintings are world-famous, the biggest names around.

So why is Sebastian's collection hidden away, out of view?

A noise from behind me makes me spin around with a yelp. It's Sebastian. "You scared me!" I blurt.

"What are you doing in here?" he asks, his face unreadable in the dim light.

"I got lost," I cover quickly. "I was looking for the kitchen. I wanted a snack."

He gives a nod. "The kitchen's this way."

I pause, lingering to look at the art. "This art is amazing," I say. "I mean, I don't know anything about it, but these guys...

These I recognize. How long have you been collecting? Is that even the right word?" I add.

"It is. And I've bought art on and off for the past ten years or so," Sebastian replies. "It's a good investment."

He moves closer to me, and I see, he's wearing a pair of grey sweatpants and a black T-shirt. You would have thought seeing him so casual would make him less imposing, but no, his posture and bearing are just as controlled and cool as ever.

"I like this one," I say, nodding to the charcoal sketch in a frame, all sharp lines.

"Picasso," Sebastian says, with a note of satisfaction in his voice. "The owner sold it to me cheap, after I bankrupted his company."

Charming.

"What about that one?" I ask, pointing to the Rothko.

Sebastian's smile grows. "That one I purchased at auction, five years ago. A Saudi prince wanted it, but I outbid him. And that one, it's the last in a collection," he adds, pointing to another painting. "There's a financier in Rome who has all the other pieces. He calls every month, begging me to sell it to him, for double, triple what it's worth."

"Why don't you?" I ask, even though I can guess the answer by now.

Sure enough, Sebastian gives a cool smile. "Because I do so enjoy hearing him beg."

I realize, there's nothing in this room that he actually enjoys. A room full of incredible art, and Sebastian wouldn't care if they were hunks of metal. They're all just trophies to him, ways of keeping score against his enemies.

What a waste.

"You must have pretty great security," I joke wryly, as I follow him out of the room. "To have all of that just hanging on the walls."

"Those are just copies," Sebastian answers immediately. "The real ones are all in secure storage, of course."

I blink at him. "So, you went through all the trouble of buying them, just to... lock them away in a vault somewhere, so nobody ever looks at them?"

"I didn't buy them because I like them," Sebastian says matter-of-factly. "I bought them because other people wanted them. And now, I have them. And they don't."

I exhale slowly. Sebastian takes 'winner take all' to a whole new level. It's no wonder he walked straight into my trap at the poker table.

The chance to take Nero's sweet, innocent girl from him must have been more tempting than any amount of cash.

He doesn't realize yet how high a price he'll pay.

Sebastian leads me down another hallway to the kitchen, and flips on a light. "What do you want?" he asks, and it takes me a second to realize, he's talking about the food, not my quest for revenge.

"It's fine, I can fix something," I say quickly, not wanting to be alone with him any longer.

Not with the memory of his kiss still lingering in my bloodstream.

"You're my guest," Sebastian says. Then, before I can react, he grips me by my waist, and lifts me to sit on the countertop.

I gasp in surprise, but he's already stepped away, moving to open the huge refrigerator.

"Sweet or savory?"

"Umm, sweet," I venture, trying to play it cool.

This is what I wanted, remember? To make a connection with the man. See all the different sides to him, so I can figure out the best strategy for his destruction. And a midnight kitchen rendezvous may not be what I expected, but I need to keep sharp.

"That's right," Sebastian muses, shooting me a look. "You left dinner early, before it was time for dessert."

The way his crisp English accent rolls over the word '*dessert*' is full of meaning. Suddenly, I realize, I'm in a thin nightgown and robe, perched up here on the counter in the dark kitchen.

Alone, and exposed.

"I kind of have a sweet tooth," I blurt, feeling nervous. "I always ate too much candy as a kid. My mom said that Halloween was like my real Christmas, you know, because of all the trick-or-treating. She would take me to the nice neighborhoods, because they had better candy. Full-size, instead of just the mini ones."

I'm babbling, I know, but at least it still fits my character. I send silent thanks to my former self when I was plotting this whole ruse. I didn't realize at the time that picking a sweet, innocent cover story would be so helpful. If I had to try and play sophisticated and worldly right now...

Well, Sebastian would see through me in a heartbeat.

As it is, he looks amused pulling out a glass dish of something that looks like chocolate mousse and strolling back over to where I'm sitting on the counter.

"I'll tell the chef you like it sweet," he says, producing a spoon. Then, he dips it into the mousse, and brings it to my mouth.

Feeding me.

My lips part in surprise, and he slips the spoon inside.

"Mmmmn," I make a noise of surprise—and then pleasure, as the rich chocolate hits my tongue. "Oh, wow," I blink. "That's amazing."

"There are some advantages to being a rich, heartless monster," Sebastian says smoothly. "A private chef is just one of them."

41

I almost choke on the next bite.

He smirks. "You think I don't know what you think of me? What they all think?"

He feeds me another spoonful before I can answer, and I swallow, my mind racing in surprise.

"Do you mind it?" I venture finally, searching his expression. He's standing so close that I could see any flicker of hesitation in his eyes.

But there is none.

"Not at all." Sebastian regards me, calm. "My reputation is an asset. Striking fear in my opponents means I have the advantage before we even meet on the battlefield."

"Still... It can't all be true, can it?" I ask.

I'm not sure what I want his answer to be, but Sebastian's lips curl in a cruel smile.

"Yes. It is. All the stories you've heard about me. Every crime or sin they blame me for. It's all true." He leans closer, to whisper in my ear. "Every last word."

I shiver at the ice in his words.

Sebastian draws back and regards me with cool look. "Hold still," he says, "You have..." He reaches out with his thumb and brushes a smear of chocolate from the edge of my lips.

Then he presses it into my mouth.

My eyes widen in surprise. Instinctively, I close my lips around him.

Sebastian's gaze flashes darker. "Good girl," he murmurs, low and possessive. "Now suck."

I feel a tremor plunge through my body at the command. My cheeks heat, but I couldn't disobey him if I tried.

I suck his thumb clean.

Sebastian doesn't look away. His eyes stay fixed on mine, holding me, watching as in the private heat of my mouth, I swirl my tongue over his thumb, tasting him.

Finally, Sebastian pulls it from my mouth with a wet pop.

Oh my God.

What is happening? I swear, my face is bright red right now, my pulse is pounding, and as for the rest of my body... My nipples are hard, pressing uncomfortably against the silk of my robe.

Sebastian's eyes skim over me, and I can tell from the smug satisfaction on his face, he sees the traitorous peaks.

"Sweet indeed..." He muses. "But I wonder..."

He places a heavy hand on each of my knees, and—still holding my gaze—slowly pushes them open.

I feel another rush of heat, caught in the command of his gaze. What is he planning now? I'm completely covered by my nightgown, but I've never felt more exposed as he deliberately parts my thighs, moving to stand in the open V.

Oh God. My core is damp, aching, and all he would have to do is slide those hands higher to touch me...

And any pretense of control would be gone forever.

With the last thread of sense in my brain, I realize, I'm on the edge of a cliff here. And there's no way I can fall off, not now.

Sebastian values what he can't have. There's a room full of trophies down the hall, proving that beyond all doubt. If I give in to him now?

He won't want me half as much. And my plan will be over, before its even begun.

With super-human control, I bring my legs closed again.

"It's late," I say, my voice coming out breathy. "I should really get to bed. My bed," I add. "Alone."

Sebastian pauses for a moment, then stands back. "Of course."

Relieved, I slide down from the counter, but my legs are unsteady, and I stumble against him.

"Easy there." Sebastian steadies me.

"Sorry."

"There's nothing to apologize for."

Sebastian doesn't release me. Instead, he presses me back against the counter, bringing me in hard against his body. So close, I can feel the thick ridge of his erection pressing against my stomach.

I gasp.

"You feel it, don't you?" he demands, his voice low. He takes my chin in one hand and tilts it up, so I have no choice but to look at him. "You see, our bodies can't lie. You can tell yourself you don't want me, protest and play the innocent all you want, but your body tells a different story."

His free hand trails down my bare neck... Over my collarbone... Barely brushing my aching breasts through the robe...

I shiver.

"That's right," Sebastian sounds a low, cruel laugh. "You're already wet for me, aren't you? Buried between those sweet thighs, your pussy feels empty. Aching. Because your body already knows, it belongs to me now."

I wrench away. "I'm not your property," I tell him, grasping at anger to ignore the truth in his words. "You bought my time, but you can never buy me."

"We'll see about that, Sparrow." Sebastian's face is unreadable. "You can fly away now, but we both know you'll be begging for my cock soon enough."

"Want to bet on it?" I retort sharply.

"It would be my pleasure." Sebastian finally smiles, and I remember, this is what he does best. Gamble with other people's lives, until the price is too high for them to pay.

Miles paid, though. With his life.

I fix Sebastian with a glare. "No," I tell him, furious—at him, and myself, for letting my guard down even for a moment.

44

I draw myself up to my full height and give him a withering stare. "I'm not another of your twisted games, so stop trying to play. It doesn't matter how much money you have; my body is not for sale."

And then I turn and stalk off to bed, ignoring the slick heat between my thighs and the way my head still spins, remembering his touch.

Fuck, I'm in trouble now.

Chapter 6

Sebastian

I watch Avery go. She's trying to act confident, walking out on me, but the skitter in her steps gives her away.

It's intoxicating to see her fight against her burgeoning desire. The flush in her cheeks, the catch in her breath.

The tantalizing peek of her stiff nipples, pebbled under her silky robe. A glimpse of her desire that leaves me hungry for more. To taste her, gorge on her, bring that pretty mouth to a desperate plea.

Patience...

I finish the chocolate dessert, imagining the day I'll lick it from her naked body. How she'll moan and writhe, that sweet voice of hers echoing in pleasure, until she finally admits the need she's been fighting.

How I'll own her, completely. What a victory that will be.

Sweeter than any check Nero Barretti could write, that's for sure. I thought I was stealing his favorite plaything away from him, but it turns out, I won something far more valuable in that poker game.

A prize even he hasn't tasted just yet.

Him, or anyone else. Because I'd wager my considerable fortune on the fact that sweet Avery is still a virgin, and an untrained one, at that. She tries to act confident, but her youth betrays her. The way she responds to my touch, the flash of confusion and resentment in her eyes when I explored her mouth, a stranger to the new sensations her body produced...

She's an innocent, through and through.

For now.

But soon, I'll strip that from her, and show her the pleasure of pure corruption.

Soon, I'll claim her as my own.

And not just as a fuck-you to Nero Barretti, either, although that will be a fine benefit, too. No, now I've glimpsed the passion that lies beneath her prim surface, simmering in those big blue eyes of hers, I'll take it as a personal challenge. I'm going to be the one to unleash the sensual goddess she has locked away inside. I can't wait to make that gorgeous voice of hers scream my name.

And I'll take my time, too. The best pleasures in life are to be savored. After all, anticipation is half the reward. Once I've conquered her, I know, I'll be moving on, looking for my next challenge. But for now? I have a whole month to enjoy Miss Carmichael's charms...

And I'll relish every moment.

I leave the kitchen, and head upstairs to my suite. The financial markets are opening in Asia, so I check a few stock prices before I see a new email come through. It's from the investigator I hired to check Avery out.

Good. Nobody gets near me for any reason without a full background check, and this girl is no exception. I've had competitors try to send women to seduce me, planning to pick up corporate secrets from pillow talk. They never succeed. Sure, I fuck them, why wouldn't I, when they're offering themselves up on a platter—and collecting a pretty penny for it too, I'm sure.

But my secrets stay buried, no matter who is sharing my bed.

Opening it up, I scan the information. Mother: Absent. Father: Deceased. A family farm... debt to the Barrettis...

It all checks out.

I'm pleased. She's clearly lived a sheltered life, a world away from the high-stakes battles and betrayals that litter my own history. And I'd be lying if I said I didn't find her naiveite tempting, a refreshing change from the jaded women that usually move in my circles—out to secure their next rich husband, or to distract them from the last one.

No, Avery is untouched by that greed and cynicism. I can tell from the way she toured the house, wide-eyed, uncomfortable in her new designer heels. But still...

There's something she's hiding from me.

It's instinct, some unconscious alert in the back of my brain. And I know better than to ignore it. Maybe it's something innocent, or maybe I'm so used to lies and deception that I assume everyone in the world must be harboring an ulterior motive.

But either way, I won't let my guard slip, not for an instant —and certainly not for some wide-eyed girl, straight off the farm.

After all, this is my empire. It doesn't matter what she might be planning, I'll take what I want from her, the way I always do.

I'm the one in control here.

And I always will be.

. . .

I don't sleep long, I never do. At four, I'm awake again to check the markets, and fire off emails to my team at Wolfe Capital. They're all awake too, if they know what's good for them. I demand total dedication from my team—and pay them handsomely for it.

After all, where else could they get a starting salary of half a million dollars—plus bonuses?

I learned a long time ago, the only way to get true loyalty is to buy it. With wealth—and fear.

And I'm generous with both of them.

After pressing business, I hit the in-home gym for an hour, running off my tension on the treadmill. I'm just stepping off, sweaty and panting, when movement on the beach below catches my eye.

It's Avery, strolling down to the water's edge. She unties her robe, letting it fall to the sand, revealing a simple white bikini.

Fuck.

Even from here, I can tell that the skimpy bikini she's wearing leaves little to the imagination. With her pale skin and dark hair, she almost shimmers in the bright sunlight.

My cock twitches, remembering how that body felt pressed against it last night.

Almost as if she senses my eyes on her, Avery turns to look back in the direction of the house. She's too far away for me to make out her expression, but my gaze darts over the swell of her barely contained breasts and her lush hips. The kind of body a man would kill to hold; to grip on tightly, as he sinks inside, riding her hard until she breaks.

Avery turns back. Then she slips into the water, leaving me standing here, my cock already hard, and my breath coming fast.

How would she take it, down on her knees?

I already know she's a girl who can follow instruction. My thumb in her mouth last night was a tantalizing preview of what's to come.

In my bathroom, I turn on the steam shower, and swiftly strip naked, stepping under the spray. I'm already gripping my cock, harder, as I imagine issuing the command.

On your knees. Hands behind your back. Swallow me down, sweetheart.

I groan, working myself faster, slick with shower gel and the hot water spray.

Has she even sucked off a man before?

Fuck, I always thought virgins were more trouble than they were worth. Why have some inexperienced girl fumble around, when you could enjoy more expert attentions?

But now, the thought of teaching her... *Training her...* I'm hard as steel, groaning in the empty bathroom. Yes, she'll be a good girl for me, follow every filthy command I give her, until she's obediently taking my cock—all the way down, swallowing every thick inch, massaging me with her tight virgin throat until I can't last another second.

And if she doesn't?

Well, she'll learn exactly how I like it, soon enough.

The idea of punishing her, marking that pale flesh with my handprints—and more—is what finally pushes me over the edge. *Fuck.* I come with a low roar, my climax surging out of me until I'm panting under the spray.

I take a deep breath, and then another, letting my crazed desire wash away. Then I rinse off, shut off the water, and emerge with a clear head, and my usual cool determination in place again.

Avery may be a tempting treat, but she's still just an amusement to me. I won't be distracted, not by anybody, and certainly not anything as simple as base lust.

My cellphone phone rings as I finish dressing. It's Rebecca Hargreaves, one of my most trusted people at the company. I've got her keeping an eye on things at Wolfe Capital while I'm out of England.

"Talk to me," I command. She knows not to waste my time with anything so trivial as small talk.

"It's Richard."

Damn it. Of course, it is. My uncle has been a constant thorn in my side.

"What now?" I demand, the pleasure of my morning diversion already a distant memory.

"He dropped by the office unexpectedly yesterday," Becca says. "Just a casual visit, but he did the rounds, shaking hands and getting some one-on-ones with key departments."

"What does he want?"

"I'm still not sure," Becca admits—even knowing I hate that answer. "It seems innocent enough. He even came by my office, chatted about my family, and the weather, as if it was no big deal at all."

"This is my uncle we're talking about. Nothing he does is innocent." I take another breath, thinking calmly. "Who did he meet?"

"Frank in Venture. Amy and Varun. The new hires in Strategy."

Top-level players at the company. And people that Richard, as a silent partner, should have no business talking to. "He's trying to undermine my authority," I say, irritated.

"Seems like it," Becca sighs. "I'd recommend you get back here ASAP and remind everyone who's boss."

That's why I like Becca. She's a straight-shooter, and I can trust her. She understands how business works.

"I'll be back tomorrow." I say shortly and hang up.

Uncle Richard...

The man is a constant threat to my power. My father's older brother, he was always jealous of what Dad managed to build. Wolfe Capital was meant to be a partnership, and Dad offered it to him as a joint venture: fifty-fifty. But Richard sneered at Dad's plans to go all-in on new tech stocks. This was the 90s, and Richard didn't want to take the risk. So he went his own way, and then watched as my father grew the investment fund to a multi-million-pound powerhouse.

Of course, my father would never hold a grudge. His brother meant the world to him. They mended fences, he gave Richard shares in the company, and even named him a trustee in the will, so when he passed, Richard stepped in as caretaker CEO of Wolfe Capital.

Until I came of age and took my rightful place as head of the company.

It should have been the end of the story, right there. But I suppose Richard got a taste of power, calling all the shots, and now he still can't let go. I've expanded our business and profits tenfold since I took control, but still, the man is nosing around in my business, whispering in the wrong ears, always out to claw back control.

If he was any other rival, I would have destroyed him a long time ago. Nobody else gets to challenge my power like this, not without paying a heavy price. But Richard is off-limits to me. Not just because he's family, either.

Because he's the one person who knows my secrets.

Secrets that would destroy me, if they ever saw the light of day.

So now I have to make sure that they stay buried.

Chapter 7

Avery

Travelling with Sebastian is like a window into another world.

I know power. I've grown up in the Barretti mafia world and saw how Nero runs things. He can walk through any door in the city and have people leaping to serve his every demand. But that's because they all fear him, watching with that look of scandal and worry in their eyes.

Sebastian Wolfe is different.

People *want* to serve him.

Everyone treats him like royalty, head turning when he walks into the room. Men look at him with admiration. Women gaze with desire. And he doesn't seem to notice any of it. From the private jet to the airfield, to the sleek town car waiting on the tarmac, he moves in a bubble of wealth and privilege with total confidence.

A bubble I'm part of too, now.

I feel a tremble of nerves as the car glides through Central London, but I try to hide it, pretending to read a magazine. Sebastian's barely spoken to me for the entire journey. He's been on his laptop, barking orders into his cellphone. It's kind of a relief, after the way things went on the island. The way he kissed me, touched me... I still feel it in my body, aware of his every movement and breath.

I'm in his territory now.

The island was just the beginning, a brief glimpse of his high-powered life. Now...

Now the real work begins.

I gaze out of the car windows at the unfamiliar city. I've never travelled much, New York City is more than enough for me, but now, I drink in the historic architecture, and new, gleaming buildings, side-by-side on leafy streets.

The car slows in a chic neighborhood, and I catch a glimpse of an impressive modern home behind huge walls, not that I expected anything different. Big windows face the street and there's a newness about the structure, as if it was built in the last few years. Its natural stone exterior is a clean white color, and its modern design fits a man like Sebastian perfectly.

The driver pulls into an underground parking structure beneath the house, where there's a collection of other expensive cars gathered. Aston Martin, Bugatti, Porsche...

I have a thing for cars, and I look at them hungrily before remembering that innocent little Avery wouldn't know a thing about driving.

I turn away, as Sebastian marches to the elevator, and we swoop upwards.

He's still scrolling on his phone, looking absorbed.

OK, so maybe I'll have a little more freedom to snoop around than I thought, if he can't even look at me.

Then the elevator doors open on the main floor, and I have to change my mind. A hulking man in a black suit is waiting for us, along with a line of other staff. The beast steps forward the second we get off the elevator, his eyes on Sebastian.

"Welcome home, sir," he says, in a thick Cockney accent.

"Leon." Sebastian nods. "This is Avery." Leon's gaze shifts to me, and it lingers curiously. "She'll be staying with me for the month."

"Got it."

"Leon is the house manager," Sebastian tells me. "He's in charge of my staff, so if you need anything, you can ask him, and he'll take care of it."

"Okay, thanks." I say, giving the man a small smile. He seems like a good person to have on my side.

Leon stares back, impassive.

"Make yourself at home." Seb doesn't wait for a reply before walking off, down the hallway to what looks like an office. He steps inside and firmly closes the door behind him.

"Come with me, ma'am, and I'll show you your room."

Leon is waiting.

"You can call me Avery," I tell him, but he doesn't crack a smile, he just heads for the
grand staircase.

I follow, looking curiously around. Just like the exterior, everything here is modern and gleaming new. High-end furniture, modern art, lots of white and black ironwork.

The second floor has an open, loft walkway, allowing me to see down in the foyer and great room below. I follow Leon down the hallway, passing gorgeous and probably priceless paintings on the walls along the way.

I wonder if these are just copies, too.

Leon leads me to at a door at the far end, revealing a spacious bedroom suite, with a bathroom, dressing room, and even a small space with a personal gym. It's decorated tastefully in more shades of white and navy, like some kind of hotel suite.

"I'll have your things brought up from the car," he says. "If you want to go anywhere, just ask for Frank. He's the driver. And this is for you, to buy whatever clothes and things you need." He produces a black credit card, with Sebastian's name on it.

I take it slowly. "Umm, what's the limit?" I ask hesitantly. "I mean, did he say what I was allowed to spend?"

Leon looks at me like I'm an idiot. "Mr. Wolfe doesn't have limits," he says, and I have to stifle a smile.

Because I sure as hell know what I'm doing for the rest of the day.

Shopping.

I take Frank, and the Benz, and hit the stores for the rest of the day. I have zero luggage to speak of, and no idea what lies ahead for me, so I'm starting from scratch here.

And every character needs the right costume.

It takes me a hot minute to get into it. I keep reaching for outfits I would wear in real life: cool leather jackets, studded boots, sharp angles, and bold cuts.

But then I remember, I'm not me anymore. I'm the Little Sparrow who's going to peck out Sebastian's eyes.

And I need to look the part.

So, I hit the designer stores on Bond Street. Gucci, St Laurent. Harrods. I buy dresses and jewelry, shoes and gowns. The totals ring up with so many zeroes, I feel faint, but soon I get into the swing of things, and every pound I spend feels like a little 'fuck you' to Sebastian.

It's dirty money, anyway. I might as well take full advantage, right?

By the time I return to the house that evening, I'm exhausted, and it takes Leon half-a-dozen trips to bring all my purchases up to my room. My expansive dressing room is now full to the brim.

And I'm betting Sebastian won't even notice the tiny dent my hundred-thousand-dollar shopping spree put in his vast fortune.

I would love to sink into a hot bath, order some food sent up to my room, and have an early night, but I know that my work is just getting started. I can't lock myself away, if I'm going to uncover Sebastian's secrets.

I need to know more. And that means spending more time with him.

I head downstairs. The door of his office is open now, and I can hear his voice coming from inside. He has company: A woman's there with him.

Unable to contain my curiosity, I step closer, lingering just back from the doorway. I can see Sebastian is seated behind his desk, and there's a woman across from him, leaning forward to hear a call that's playing on the cellphone speaker. I crane to see more of her. She's in her thirties, dressed in business casual, but expensive: tailored silk pants and a creamy blouse, with lots of statement gold jewelry. Her brown hair is in a chic bob, and she's wearing bold lipstick. Her features are pretty plain, but she's put together and stylish, and has a confident look about her.

Who is she to Sebastian?

I do a quick assessment of the two of them, taking in the space between them and the way that both of their attention is focused on the phone and some paperwork on the desk in front of them, not each other. I can't be sure, but this seems like a business associate, maybe a friend since she's in his home. But I don't sense any sexual tension in the air.

Good. I don't need any competition for his attention in that area.

"I don't care if the owner is reluctant. I'm not giving up until I get what I want, and I want that company." Sebastian says, sounding annoyed.

"If it comes down to it, we have ways of forcing his hand," the woman across from Sebastian chimes in. "He'll lose everything, but that's his own fault if he won't be agreeable."

"Let's try the easy route first," the man's voice on the speakerphone says. "You know how it is in business. Sometimes a little charm goes along way."

"You have twenty-four hours, then we go full force. Have the lawyers prepare the filings." Sebastian replies, not looking convinced. He suddenly glances up and sees me standing there. "We're done here. I'll touch base with you tomorrow."

He ends the call, and by now, the woman has noticed me as well. I feel her eyes on me, curious.

Clearly, Sebastian doesn't invite women into his home very often.

"Becca, this is Avery." Sebastian makes a clipped introduction. "Becca Hargreaves works with me at Wolfe Capital."

"Hi," I send her a big smile.

She barely stretches her lips in return.

Sebastian doesn't notice. He's checking his phone. "I have to get to the Lawton meeting."

She nods, already pulling a file from her large, designer briefcase. "I have the data here. The main highlights are summarized on the cover sheet."

Sebastian doesn't thank her; he just takes the file as they both exit the office. He closes the door behind them, and I swallow my disappointment.

If that's where his business action is, I'm going to want to take a look.

Sebastian exits, and I turn—and find Becca watching me. I paste on a big smile. "Do you want a drink?" I offer brightly.

"Iced tea—no, wait, you Brits only like your tea hot, with milk and sugar."

"I could use some water," Becca replies, still looking like she wants to figure me out.

The feeling's mutual.

"Great!" I beam, all smiles, and make my way to the massive chef's kitchen, with views onto the back gardens. "Now, if I can just figure out where the fridge is..." I start, looking at the banks of matching built-in cabinets.

Becca doesn't hesitate, she goes straight for the middle row, and opens it to reveal the hidden refrigerator. "Wow, thanks," I smile again, playing the ditsy American girl. "I'm still trying not to get lost here."

She passes me a bottle of San Pellegrino. "I'm sure you'll learn, soon enough."

"So, you and Sebastian must know each other pretty well. Have you worked together for a long time?" I ask, trying to seem as friendly as possible.

But her mood stays cool. "Nearly a decade. And you? Do you know him well?"

As well as I can, considering I'm obsessed with destroying him.

"We just met a couple of days ago," I trill, with a little giggle. "It's all been a bit of a whirlwind!"

Becca looks like she wants to roll her eyes, and why wouldn't she? She's the high-powered business exec, and I'm just her boss's latest piece of arm candy. "That's just how Sebastian operates. He doesn't wait around for anything," she says, like I'm a child.

"I'm beginning to see." I reply, still sunny. "He's quite a guy, don't you think?"

"Yes." Becca replies evenly.

OK, so she's not exactly Miss Gossip, but that's OK. I'm

going to need allies for my mission, and Becca is as well placed as anyone to give me the inside scoop on Sebastian.

Whether she knows it yet or not.

"Well, I won't keep you," I say with a smile. "I'm sure you have a ton of important work waiting. I'm so impressed," I add. "Sebastian clearly values your advice. And we know he doesn't put up with any bullshit."

That makes her look a little warmer. "No, he doesn't. He has impeccable instincts," she adds. "And he's a masterful judge of character. Nobody can get one over on him."

Is that a warning?

I pretend like I don't even notice. "You know, we should do lunch sometime! Wouldn't that be fun?"

"Delightful," Becca says dryly.

"Awesome!" I clap, getting into this whole bimbo act. "Maybe I can get your number?"

She gives me a look. "I'll have my assistant set something up."

"Great."

I show her out, and resolve to keep an eye on her. She was right about one thing: Sebastian doesn't suffer fools, which means that after ten years working at Wolfe Capital, Becca must be a force to be reckoned with.

She could be a great ally for me... or a formidable enemy.

"Ma'am," Leon's voice comes from directly behind me, and I whirl around to see him standing there. "Mr. Wolfe has made dinner reservations. The driver will be here to get you at seven."

It's not an invitation, it's an order.

"Thanks," I tell him, only to have him leave without another word. Real friendly bunch, Sebastian has here.

So, dinner...

I think hard, wondering which sweet, demure outfit I should wear tonight.

Then I stop. I've been on the defensive since the night we met. Reacting to *his* moves, trying to figure out *his* next step.

Overwhelmed by each new move of his subtle seduction.

It's time I turned the tables and took back the upper hand. Tonight, I'm going to have him panting after *me*.

And prove I have value beyond just a gambling prize.

Chapter 8

Avery

I walk into the restaurant with my head held high—even though I'm a tangle of nerves beneath this silk of my designer dress. I can tell the place is exclusive from the subtle entryway, and the fact there's no sign marking the entrance, just a man in uniform ready to open the door and whisk me inside the dim, clubby atmosphere.

I look around. It's all dark leather and stylish people glittering under the chandeliers. Not my usual hangout, that's for sure.

But I'm a long way from home.

"Sparrow."

I turn at the sound of Sebastian's voice. He greets me in the foyer, and his eyes sweep down the length of my body. I'm wearing a midnight blue silk cocktail dress that falls over my curves like water, embellished with tiny crystals that gleam under the lights. I styled my hair down, in loose waves, with shimmering natural makeup, and high-heeled strappy sandals. I was aiming for the classic movie star look, and watching Sebastian's eyes flash with lust, I know I've made the right move.

"You look gorgeous," he murmurs, and I give a bashful smile.

"Thank you."

"Mr. Wolfe, your table is ready," the hostess says, gazing at him in awe.

And she's not the only one. As we're led through the restaurant, people hush their conversation to watch, heads turning to see us pass. When we get to the table the hostess has set aside for us, I move forward to sit down, but Sebastian shakes his head.

"No," he says simply.

"Ex... Excuse me?" the hostess looks terrified.

"This isn't my usual table." Sebastian's tone is perfectly even, but it's like a bomb just went off from the way the woman gasps.

"I'm so sorry, I didn't realize."

"I prefer to sit there." Sebastian nods to a table in the very middle of the room. Where everyone can see. It's already occupied by an older couple, halfway through dinner, but to my surprise, the man immediately gets to his feet.

"We're happy to move," he says quickly.

"That's very kind of you," Sebastian says coolly.

"It's no trouble. No trouble at all!" The man, who must be twice Sebastian's age, and wealthy too, judging from his suit and expensive watch, practically grovels to step aside. "Mabel, come on, get out of their way."

There's a rush of activity as the waitstaff descend, and barely a moment later, we're seated at the freshened table, while the man and his wife are moved across the room.

"Much better, don't you think?" Sebastian says. He orders an expensive bottle of wine for us to share, and I wait until the hostess leaves us alone to say anything.

"The other table would have been fine," I say quietly.

"I'm sure it would have. But what fun would that be?" Sebastian replies, with a smirk of satisfaction. And then I realize—he didn't really care about the table, he just felt like proving he was the most important man in the room.

"That was kind of an asshole move," I can't help saying. "I would have thought only small, insecure men worry about things like a table position."

His eyes flash up, and I immediately regret it. *So much for playing sweet and docile.* But then Sebastian's mouth spreads in a smile.

"A very asshole move," he agrees, looking amused. "And you're right, I don't give a damn about the table. But the man who just moved for us? He's a businessman, on the board of a company I'm considering buying. I wondered what kind of reception I'd get, whether they'd put up a fight at all. And now I know. In fact, I'm going to reduce my bid by fifty percent, since clearly, he has no backbone at all. Imagine, offering to let someone walk all over you the way he just did."

Sebastian scowls in clear disdain, and I realize something. That for all the appeal of sweet Avery's innocent act, he respects people who show strength. Who stand up to him, talk back.

Good.

"Let's not devote another minute to insignificant people," Sebastian continues, giving me a slow, assessing look. "Not with far more interesting things to enjoy tonight."

My skin tingles where his gaze lands, as if it's a physical touch.

"So, what's good here?" I ask brightly, reaching for the menu. "I'm hungry."

"That's right," Sebastian smiles. "I'll have to tell the chef to stock the kitchen at home for your midnight snacks."

His eyes meet mine, and I blush, hit by the sensual memory

of him feeding me that chocolate mousse. His hands gripping my knees.

His thumb in my mouth.

Heat spirals through me. "Wow. Steak and lobster, this place is fancy," I blurt, as a distraction. "But I think there's something wrong with my menu. There are no prices on it."

Sebastian chuckles, as if charmed. "You really have been sheltered," he says. "I forget, you're a long way from home."

"I'm sorry," I drop my eyes again, all bashful innocence. "You're probably used to dating all these sophisticated women."

"I am," he replies. "But I'm rather enjoying the change. Don't worry," he reassures me. "I'll take care of everything."

Our waitress arrives with our wine. Opening the bottle, she pours a sample for Sebastian to try. When he nods approvingly, she puts some in each of our glasses. I test it out while Sebastian orders for both of us, rattling off a long list of luxurious-sounding dishes. "Tell Anton to prepare it the way I like," he finishes, handing our menus back.

"Of course, Mr. Wolfe."

She leaves, and we're alone again. I try not to gulp my wine. I need to keep my wits sharp, I know. "You seem at home here," I notice. "Was it hard, learning how to fit in with these people?"

Sebastian looks surprised. "What do you mean?"

"You mentioned that your dad built the company from nothing. I figured that means you didn't grow up wealthy."

Sebastian seems pleased. "You surprise me yet again."

"You don't think I'm capable of an insightful question?" I ask, keeping my voice teasing.

He smiles. "I didn't say that." He sips his wine before answering. "And no, I didn't grow up with money, or privilege. My mother worked as a secretary, and my father was from a working-class background, too. But he had ambition, and brains." Sebastian's voice is admiring. "He worked a dozen different jobs and saved every penny to start the business. I was twelve, when things really took off. They sent me to a fancy boarding school," he adds. "And it was... educational, certainly." His smile twists. "But I learned quickly how the social system works. It's all about dominance. Show no fear, be merciless. There's no room for sentiment or emotions if you want to get ahead."

"I'm sorry," I tell him.

He blinks. "Why?"

"Well, it doesn't sound like it was much fun."

He gives a dry laugh. "That school taught me everything I needed to know. And I've never looked back."

Okaay.

Clearly, this boarding school was more of a Slytherin vibe. But I can see, Sebastian is starting to relax and open up to me, so I'll take any information as a win.

It doesn't take long for the food to come, and it's delicious. I've never had food prepared by a five-star chef, and I can see that I've been missing out. I'm halfway through my meal when I look up, feeling eyes on me. They're not Sebastian's.

There's a man and woman approaching our table, and the woman's eyes are locked on me. I see curiosity burning in their depths.

The couple is older, maybe in their sixties, and impeccably dressed. Diamonds are draped around the woman's neck and hanging from her earlobes. The man's got a broad frame and thick grey hair, wearing a thousand-dollar suit. These people must be a part of Sebastian's world.

As they stop at our table, I learn just how right I am about that.

"Mum," Sebastian stands and politely kisses her on the cheek.

Mum?

I snap to attention. I can't believe my luck, to be meeting his family so soon.

Families are always full of secrets.

Pulling away from his mom, Sebastian nods at the man with her. "Uncle Richard."

His tone is cool, and it takes me a minute to process the situation. Because the way his mother is standing close to the man, a hand on his arm... It makes me think that they are a couple.

His mom... and his uncle?

"Sebastian, it's good to see you," his uncle says, too loud. "I have to say, I'm surprised. I heard that you were still out of town, having your fun." He gives a booming laugh.

"It was just a small vacation," Sebastian replies. "But I'm back to work now."

I'm positive I'm missing something here. Sebastian's voice is now even cooler, even if his words are friendly enough.

"Aren't you going to introduce us to your friend?" Sebastian's mother asks, giving me an appraising look.

"Avery, this is my mother, Trudy," he says, providing no other explanation for who I am. That's probably for the best. 'The woman I won and kidnapped from a poker game' isn't exactly the kind of thing you'd share with your parents.

"It's nice to meet you, dear," Trudy says, her smile bright. She seems genuinely delighted. "We so rarely get to meet any of Sebastian's friends."

Maybe because he's incapable of real, human relationships?

"It's great to meet you, too," I smile back.

"An American, how lovely. Have you been in England for long?" she asks.

"Not at all. I'm looking forward to doing some sightseeing," I add.

"Well in that case, the two of you should come visit us in

the country sometime," Richard suggests. "We'd love to have you."

Us. We. Yeah, these two are definitely a couple.

Weird.

"Perhaps," Sebastian replies vaguely. "I'll have to see about my schedule."

"Well, you know what they always say," Richard jokes. "All work and no play, and all that jazz." He chortles again, and Trudy titters along, too. "Well, lovely meeting you, Avery. Keep an eye out for my nephew, he's a real heartbreaker," he adds with a wink, before the two of them leave.

Wow. I have about a million questions, but Sebastian changes the subject right away, almost as if he's trying to avoid any conversation about those two. "If you're interested in seeing the city, I can hire a guide for you."

"Oh, that's OK." I reply. "I like to just wander, getting lost. It's the best way to explore."

He nods, but still looks tense. I smile along, and chat inanely about exploring the city, but inside, I file the information away for later.

Something tells me, his family is a pressure point. And I mean to test them all—until he's howling in pain.

After dinner, we don't go home. Instead, a car whisks us through London, to an older neighborhood, where another uniformed valet is waiting outside another unmarked door. This time, it's some kind of exclusive club, with a long bar area, dim velvet booths, and a young, stylish clientele. Music is playing, too loud to really talk, and it's busy enough that I can relax.

I'm relieved. Being alone with Sebastian is a dangerous thing, and after the time we spent on the island together, I know he's determined to seduce me. I need to keep him at arm's length for as long as possible so he doesn't lose interest in me.

And I don't lose control, seduced by his magnetic touch.

"You like it?" Sebastian asks, seeing me look curiously around.

"I guess. I'm not really into nightlife," I lie. I've kept the Barretti clubs running like clockwork since the day I turned eighteen, but that was a whole different world.

Sebastian orders us both drinks at the bar, and then is intercepted by a couple of finance bros.

"You see the FTSE tremble over those rate hikes?" one asks, ignoring me.

"I'm not worried," Sebastian shrugs. "I've hedged enough."

"Of course you have," the other laughs, too eager. "Nobody gets around you."

I sit there, listening. I try to pick up anything that might be useful to me, but I soon realize, it's just macho bragging—the two guys trying to impress Sebastian while he calmly sips his drink.

"I'm telling you; you've got to go big on pharma next quarter," one of them is urging him. "I've got my eye on Ashford Pharmaceuticals, they're going to go through the roof with a little nudge."

"And nobody fucks like those pharma rep girls," the other whoops.

I have to force myself not to react to their idiot comments. Sebastian is friends with these morons?

"Ashford is a waste of time," Sebastian says, sounding bored. "I took a look, but I'm not impressed."

"That's because they're still in the trial phase of their new drug," the guy says eagerly. "I have the inside track from a researcher there, they're going to blow everyone away when they announce..."

As the guy blabbers on about his top-secret source, Sebastian meets my eyes, and gives me the smallest hint of a smile.

He's playing games again.

I have to control my expression again, this time to keep from laughing. Of course. He would never waste his time with assholes like this unless there was some angle to be played, so I'm guessing he's stringing them along to get more information —which he'll probably use to turn around and screw them over.

It unnerves me to realize I already know him this well.

"Excuse me," I murmur, slipping out of the booth. Nobody bothers to acknowledge me as I cross the room and go find the bathroom.

It's large and luxurious, of course, like everything in Sebastian's world. Maybe I'll get used to it soon, but for now, I still feel like an interloper, out of place beneath all my new designer clothes, and if anyone looks too closely, I'll be exposed.

Get it together, I tell myself in the mirror. Sebastian said it himself, didn't he? There's no room for sentiment or emotion. I need to stop thinking of myself as a fish out of water.

You're an assassin, behind enemy lines.

The stalls are separate from the sinks, but as I'm reapplying my lipstick, I hear a voice call out.

"Hello? Is anyone in here?"

I furrow my brow and turn in the direction of the stalls. "Uh... Yeah?"

"Oh, thank God. *Please* tell my you're a better prepared woman than I am and have a tampon in your purse. I'll even use a pad if I must."

I smile. "Let me check."

My purse is small, so it doesn't take me long to find a single tampon that I tucked into a side pocket in case of emergency.

"I have one," I say, going further back into the section

where the stalls are. A woman's hand sticks out from under one of them, and I go toward it, handing it over.

"Thank God. You're a real lifesaver. You know that?"

"Just call me superwoman."

"Well, I'm Lulu." The voice says.

"Avery," I say. I turn to start to head back to the sinks when the toilet flushes and the door opens. The woman that walks out is a petite blonde in her twenties. She's wearing the same kind of chic outfit as the other women here tonight, but her hair is a mass of blonde curls, and there's a lively sparkle in her eyes.

"Well, Avery, I think I owe you a drink. And my firstborn. I'm not too clear about the rules of girl-code." She grins, friendly, and I can't help smiling back.

"That's okay," I laugh. "On both things." As much as I'd like to chat with a potential new friend, I can't lose sight of my purpose here. "I better get back to my... date."

"Didn't I see you come in with Sebastian Wolfe?"

I pause. "You know him?"

"Who doesn't?" Lulu rolls her eyes, grinning. "The man is like the most eligible bachelor in London. No, really, the *Gazette* ran a whole rankings list, he came out on top."

"I'm sure he'd be thrilled," I reply dryly, and she laughs.

"So, what's he like?" Lulu asks, her eyes widening. "I've always wondered if he really is as cutthroat and serious as everyone says. Or is he a softie, under those designer suits?"

I pause, considering my answer. The woman seems nice, definitely friendly, but there's something behind her eager questions. Like they're not so casual as she's making it seem.

I should recognize the signs. I've been playing a part myself for the last few days.

"He's impatient," I say vaguely. "So, I better get back to him. It was nice meeting you, though."

"You too!" Lulu beams, not seeming bothered by my reply. "And thank you again, I owe you!"

I head back out to the club. It's starting to get a little more crowded, and I weave my way through people to get back to Sebastian. I'm halfway across the room when a random guy catches my arm.

"Hello, baby." He gives me a creepy look from head to toe. "Buy you a drink?"

"No thanks," I say flatly, trying to sidestep him. He follows.

"Aww, c'mon. Loosen up a little, why don't you?"

"Again, no thanks." I glare. He just laughs, sliding an arm around me—and moving his hand to rest on my ass.

"Hard to get, I like it!"

He squeezes.

Motherfucker.

I whirl around, ready to slam his face into the nearest solid surface, and hell, maybe stamp on his puny dick for good measure, when I see a flash of movement across the room. Sebastian, heading straight for us.

And then I remember: I'm supposed to be helpless. Innocent. Not the girl who was raised in bad neighborhoods, telling assholes exactly where they could shove it.

So I just give a tiny push at the guy's chest. Which of course, does nothing, except make him laugh. His hand stays resting on my ass—until Sebastian is at my side, faster than I would have thought possible.

Right away, the guy backs off. "Shit, Wolfe, sorry," he stammers, taking in Sebastian's murderous glare. "I didn't realize she was with you."

And otherwise, groping me would have been fair game? Lovely.

"She is." Sebastian is icy, casually moving between us. He places a possessive arm around me. "And you are?"

"N-nobody."

"Well, Mr. Nobody, I'm afraid your drab little life is about to get a little more interesting." Sebastian's voice is low, but deadly. He moves closer, looming over the guy, who's pretty much shaking in his designer loafers. "Because you tried to take my property, so now, I'm going to take yours. Your job, your home, your pathetic excuse for self-respect. It'll take me all of two minutes to destroy your entire world. In fact, I won't even bother myself, I'll have an assistant do it. And when you're left with all that nothing, the wreckage of everything you've ever tried to build, I want you to ask yourself, was it worth it? To touch something that you could never hope to possess? I do hope so."

The man gapes, terrified.

Sebastian turns back to me, as casual as he's just caught up with an old friend. "Let's go."

I'm silent during the car ride back to his place, my mind racing. I've only spent one evening with Sebastian, but it's told me plenty. This man is every bit as heartless and commanding as I thought, and he wields that power like a weapon. Without hesitation. Ready to undercut and destroy anyone who ever dares of crossing him.

He wasn't concerned about me, when that guy put his hands on me. He was offended that anyone would dare try and take something that belongs to him.

Is that what happened to Miles? I wonder. Did he accidentally offend Sebastian somehow, and get embroiled in his gambling games? Or was he just a pawn in a bigger game, a way to hurt Nero, to send a message that Sebastian could destroy anyone he liked?

All the way to an early grave.

Back at the house, I can't wait to get away from him—and fall into bed and sleep, but Sebastian stops me on the stairs.

"The night's not over yet. Come have a nightcap with me."

"I'm tired," I back away.

"Yes, but I paid ten million dollars for the pleasure of your company, and I plan on enjoying it." Sebastian regards me with a cool, unreadable smile. "One drink," he demands.

"Fine," I murmur, realizing I don't have much of a choice. "One drink."

I just hope that's all he wants from me tonight.

Chapter 9

Avery

Sebastian leads me to the back of the house, where a huge glass-walled atrium looks out on the dark gardens beyond. Even the double-height ceiling is made of glass, and I can see the blanket of stars overhead.

Sebastian crosses to the far side of the room and opens just two windows, allowing a light breeze to flow through, carrying the scent of flowering jasmine.

I stifle a sigh. The setting would be romantic, with anyone else.

As it is, I'm on guard, wary over Sebastian's next move. He goes to fix us drinks at the retro-style bar, while I take a seat on one of the elegant couches.

"Wine or whiskey?" Sebastian asks, looking over at me.

I pause. I've been pretending for days. Surely a drink won't blow my cover with him?

"Whiskey. Thanks."

Sebastian pours two, from what I'm sure is an expensive bottle. He hands me one, then takes a seat opposite me.

We sit there in silence.

I sip my drink, appreciating the burn of alcohol in my throat. It's a fine brand, dark and smoky.

Finally, Sebastian gives a low chuckle.

"You know, I'm not the big bad wolf. I won't bite." There's a beat of silence, and he adds. "Unless you're into that sort of thing."

The smile he sends me is the definition of 'wolfish,' but I won't relax so easily.

"Can you blame me for being on my guard?" I ask lightly, careful to keep my tone playful and teasing to balance the truth in my words. "You did technically kidnap me, after all."

Sebastian smiles, as if amused. "You're right. What would make you feel more at ease?"

I don't know, how about your total ruin?

I give a little shrug. "I guess... I don't really know you at all."

"So, let's fix that," Sebastian sits back. "Ask me anything."

"Anything?" I echo, giving him a dubious look.

"Why not?" Sebastian takes a sip. "Do I seem like a man with something to hide?"

I can't help smirking at that. But I sober up quickly when all the questions that come to mind are about Miles.

Why did you bring him into your twisted games, when he was a good man? Couldn't you see, he could never afford the high stakes you were playing?

Do you even care that he's dead now, because of you?

I fight back the bitter shock of grief. I have to be focused now and use the opening Sebastian has given me to develop some kind of bond. He thinks of me as a shiny trophy right now.

I need him to see me as a woman. Want me as more than just a prize.

So, I take another sip of my drink, and fix him with a mischievous look. "Tell me about your first kiss."

Sebastian arches an eyebrow, and chuckles. "You know, given the opportunity, some people would have asked me for stock tips," he points out.

"I don't care about your money," I say honestly.

He looks at me. "No, I don't think you do." Sebastian seems a little surprised. "But what it is you do care about, I haven't figured out just yet."

I flush, uncomfortable. *If he knew what I was thinking... What I was planning for him...* "Well, right now, I care about this kiss story," I say lightly.

He gives a chuckle. "Well... I had my first kiss when I was twelve years old," he says, swirling whiskey around his glass. "Katie Pearman. She was my best friend's stepsister, probably the prettiest girl I'd ever seen back then," he adds, with a nostalgic look. "I was at my friend's house during the summer, swimming in the pool, and he went inside to get a drink. While I was alone with Katie, I decided to try some flirting that I'd picked up from a film. I can't even remember what it was now, but I'm sure it involved some awkward compliments and an attempt to be witty."

"I can't imagine you like that," I say, and it's the truth. A young, innocent Sebastian Wolfe isn't easy to picture. He's so far beyond that now.

"I told you, the life I lead now requires confidence and dominance, but I was still learning to be that person. Anyway, it somehow worked, and I got my first kiss out of the bargain. Or maybe she just took pity on me," he adds. "Either way, I felt like a king."

"Did she break your heart?" I ask, teasingly.

He smiles. "Hardly. If you know anything about twelve-year-old boys, you can probably figure out that I was lusting after someone else as soon as it was over."

"Ah, so you're the heartbreaker. Always after your next conquest."

He smiles. "There's nothing like the thrill of the chase."

He's right. Sitting here now with him, I feel a curious sense of power. He thinks he has me all figured out, but he has no idea what's coming for him.

The hell I'm going to rain down on him, whenever I spy my chance.

"Now it's my turn to ask a question." Sebastian announces, giving me a slow, assessing look.

I laugh. "I don't recall that was our deal."

He shrugs. "My house. My whiskey. My ten million. Let's say that I make the rules in this situation."

I sip my drink and pretend to think about it. "Well, it is good whiskey," I say, with a flirty smile. "Go ahead."

I don't know what Sebastian will ask, and I'm prepared to lie through my teeth, but when his question comes, it's an easy one.

"Who taught you to play the piano?"

I exhale in relief. "My dad," I answer honestly. "He loved music and wanted to share it with me. Nothing professional," I add. "He just liked to jam sometimes."

"And the singing?" Sebastian asks.

"That's two questions." I tease. "Shouldn't it be my turn to ask another?"

"Think of it as the second part," he smiles.

I giggle. "I wasn't never really taught to sing. I just love doing it. For myself, just for fun."

"You never wanted to pursue it, as a career?"

"God, no," I blurt. "I'm not brave enough to sing in front of anyone else. I'm not meant for the spotlight," I say firmly.

"Having everyone staring at me?" I shudder. "No, thank you."

Sebastian slowly gets up and moves to sit beside me. I catch my breath, unnerved to suddenly have him so close.

"People stare at you even without a spotlight," he says in a low voice, reaching out to brush hair from my cheek. His fingertips graze my skin, and I shiver from the burning touch. "You're beautiful. When you walk into a room, everyone watches. I'm sure you have men lined up for you."

I shake my head, flushing. "No. I never even had a real boyfriend."

I don't mean to say that. It just slips out. I know it's what he wants to hear, but I don't like that I just revealed that part of myself to him. I feel exposed.

Sure enough, Sebastian's gaze is fixed on me, more intent than ever. "I find that hard to believe. No boys, back at the farm?"

I shake my head. "I wasn't interested," I say, honestly. "They were all just kids, playing around. Not... a real man."

My eyes drop to my lap. Again, I've said too much. Because it's true. I never took other guys seriously, because I was waiting for Miles. He was the only one I wanted, and now...?

Now I feel way out of my depth. Because Sebastian may be cold, and heartless, and the villain I've sworn to destroy.

But he's all man.

The way he sits beside me, with ease and confidence. The arrogance of his attitude. The confidence in his touch, his glance.

His kiss.

I hate myself for it, but my body is aware of him like nobody else. Like it's already programmed to respond to his masculine command, to remember the wicked temptation of his touch.

My pulse beats faster, and there's a moment of thick silence before Sebastian speaks again.

"Look at me, Sparrow," he says softly. I don't want to, not when my skin is prickling into goosebumps of anticipation like this, but Sebastian tilts my chin up, leaving me no choice.

His eyes burn into me, full of possessive heat. "Tell me... Are you a virgin?"

I gulp, unsure how to answer. Would it be better to lie or tell the truth? What would he want to hear?

"Yes," I whisper, hoping that I'm making the right choice.

I immediately know that I said the right thing. His smile turns devilish, and he traces a finger down my bare arm. I shiver in response to the light touch.

"No wonder you're such a nervous little bird," he murmurs. He's so close now, and I feel heat pooling in the pit of my stomach.

"I'm not—" I start to lie, but he cuts me off.

"Don't worry," he says, his voice thick. "I'll teach you. I'll teach you everything this body can do."

And as I'm reeling from the promise, he kisses me.

Oh.

His lips are soft but determined, and he moves them against mine in a slow, sensual dance.

I sway against him, overwhelmed by the rush of sensation. My body tightens, and I find myself kissing him back, my lips molded to his.

Sebastian makes a noise of appreciation, slowly tipping me back into the cushions as the kiss deepens.

I go, willingly. I can tell myself it's part of my plan, but logic is slipping from my mind under this sensual onslaught; Sebastian's tongue sliding into my mouth, as his hands glide softly over me, tracing a path over my hips, sinking into my hair, skimming over my chest—

I gasp against his mouth as his thumb brushes my breast, bare beneath the silk. Pleasure blossoms, and every nerve ending in my body sparks to life. Sebastian caresses it again, bringing my nipple to a stiff, aching peak, and God, and I feel wetness gathering between my thighs.

More. I want more.

As if hearing my silent plea, Sebastian releases my mouth, and trails kisses along the side of my neck, his hands guiding me to lay back on the couch. His weight presses me down, and the feeling is incredible. I'm pinned beneath him, lost to the pleasure of his soft caress and slowly wondering tongue as he laps against my delicate skin.

I want it. I want him.

I feel drunk, but I know that I can't excuse this on alcohol. I wish I could just blame this dark desire on the whiskey, but the truth is that I'm intoxicated by his touch. I've never felt like this before, never shuddered for a man in this way.

It's part of the plan.

I cling to that thought as he nips at the place where my neck and shoulder meet, making me moan out loud. It's part of my game, that's all.

It doesn't matter that I like it. Want it.

Ache for it.

Sebastian's hands move to my breasts, cupping them through the silk material of my dress. I shudder again, pressing into his palms. "Has anyone ever touched you here?"

His voice is a whisper in my ear, so sensual and full of promise.

"No," I moan again, as he pulls down the thin straps of my dress, gently slipping the fabric down until my breasts are exposed to him: stiff and eager under his hungry gaze.

"Beautiful," Sebastian murmurs. Then he leans in, using his tongue to trace around one stiff, pebbled nipple.

I gasp, shocked by the rush of sensation. He smiles against me as he licks again, slowly swirling, lapping over each breast, squeezing and toying with his hands until I'm moaning, for what, I'm not sure.

And then he closes his lips around one aching nipple, and sucks.

I bite back a yelp of surprise—and pleasure. Sebastian sucks harder, and then nips me lightly with his teeth.

Oh God. The mix of unfamiliar pain and pleasure sends me reeling. My thighs clench and release as I grow desperate for some kind of friction between my legs.

But Sebastian knows exactly what he's doing. As he turns his attention to my other breast, he moves a hand down between my thighs, rubbing me softly through the dress.

Yes. Oh. There.

I moan loudly, bucking eagerly against his hand.

"And here?" Sebastian lifts his head and fixes me with a smoldering look, as his fingertips slowly stroke and circle my taut bud through the layers of silk. "Has anyone ever touched you here?"

I shake my head quickly, face flushed and burning.

"Use your words, Avery," he says, and the command in his voice just makes me hotter.

"No," I gasp quickly, not wanting him to stop. "No one. Until you."

His eyes are so dark they look almost black in the low lighting. "Has anyone ever made you come?"

I gulp, my stomach swooping in anticipation. "No."

Sebastian's smile turns triumphant. "Then I'll be the first."

He moves until he's kneeling on the floor beside the couch. I can only stare at him with wide eyes as he takes my legs and pulls them over to him, so that I'm draped over the side of the couch.

"Look at you," Sebastian's voice is a growl, as he settles between my thighs. "You don't even know what you need just yet, but you can bet, I'm going to give it to you." He rucks my dress up, until it's gathered at my hips, then pushes my legs apart, the way he did in the kitchens that night.

But this time, he's eye-level with my soaked panties. He chuckles, seeing their wetness. "Oh, my sweet sparrow," Sebastian says, giving me a knowing look. "You're so ready to learn."

I feel my cheeks grow hotter and I instinctively move to shut my thighs, but Sebastian stops me, holding them firmly. Forcing them open.

"No, no," he tells me, a warning note in his voice. "You can't hide this from me now. Not when I've seen how juicy you are. Now lie back and let me have a taste."

He presses me back into the pillows, and I go light-headed. I feel him make quick work discarding my panties, and then he's draping my legs over his shoulders and leaning in, his breath hot against me.

I clutch the cushions, trembling in anticipation

I can't believe this is happening, but God, I need it. Need something to stop this ache he's sparked inside me, a deep hunger I've never felt before.

The first thing I feel is a soft kiss to my inner thigh. It's sensual and soft and strangely comforting.

Then his tongue is at my core, licking up my slick center. My breath hitches, and my eyes go wide, staring up at the stars as he laps and swirls over my clit.

Fuck.

It's incredible. I feel my legs tighten around his head automatically as I arch off the couch, but Sebastian just shoves me down again, pressing me into the pillows, pinning me in place.

"Stay down," he growls, all pretense at gentleness gone now as his mouth latches onto my clit and he plain devours me.

I cry out, reeling. God, I've never felt anything like this before. He's relentless, lapping at me, probing my pussy with his tongue and sending waves of pleasure through my body. I couldn't resist it if I tried, instinct and physical reaction has completely taken over, and I don't let myself think about who this is and why I shouldn't let myself get so swept up in the passion he ignites inside of me.

All I can do is give in to it.

"That's right," Sebastian lifts his head long enough to watch me writhe. He presses one finger inside me, and then another, stretching me into another shocked moan. "Shhh, you can take it."

I flex around him, feeling a wave of something begin to rise. I moan again, meeting his eyes, mouth open in a silent plea. Sebastian flexes his fingers inside me, watching with a cool victory in his gaze. "There you go. You need to be filled, don't you? Make that ache go away."

I buck against his hand in answer, and he rewards me by plunging his fingers deeper. Thicker. "Oh God!"

This time, I do cry out, clenching hard, and Sebastian growls. "Dammit, you're so tight."

He flexes again, and I sob, grasping to hold on to something, pleasure twisting tighter deep inside. "Please..." I find myself begging.

He smiles down at me. "Close, aren't you? So close..."

I nod, eager, moaning out loud.

"Look at you, taking my fingers so well." Sebastian muses, thrusting them into me again, flexing them deep. He finds some spot inside me, somewhere high against my walls, and rubs me there, making the pleasure crest. I gasp and moan, right there on the edge of something, desperate for that last push over the edge.

"Now be a good girl for me and come."

Sebastian closes his lips around my clit and sucks, and just like that, my body shatters. I scream through my climax, arching up off the couch with the force of my pleasure as it rocks through me in sharp, desperate waves.

Holy shit.

I gasp for air, reeling. I've never come like that in my life before, not even close.

Sebastian pulls my skirt down and gets to his feet.

"That was just your first lesson," he says, looking down at me with satisfaction in his gaze. "I'm going to teach you everything, my Little Sparrow. I'll get you nice and ready for my cock."

He bends down to press a kiss to my forehead as I lie there, trying to process what just happened.

"Goodnight," he says before walking out.

I lay there in a daze, staring at the stars overhead. The wild pleasure is already fading from my veins, and now all I feel is crushing guilt and shame rush to take its place.

What did I just do?

I knew at the start of my quest for vengeance that I would have to be intimate with Sebastian. Use my body to get close to him. Endure his touch. Suffer through sex as a means to an end.

But I never expected to want him like this.

How could I feel desire for a man I loathe? Whatever my head knows, my body isn't listening. It's ignoring all the hundreds of reasons I should be disgusted by Sebastian, not half-naked on his couch, begging for more.

Be a good girl for me...

I shiver at the memory of his filthy words, lust igniting all over again.

Dammit.

How the hell can I let this monster make me feel this way?

Chapter 10

Avery

I barely sleep a wink. I keep replaying what happened with Sebastian in the atrium, filled with self-loathing and shame.

I feel weak, and knowing that he's in the bedroom down the hall doesn't help. Maybe it was foolish to think that I could do this and stay detached. All I know is that I've lost control of this situation, and that's a serious problem. I only have a month to find a way to destroy this man, and almost a week has passed me by already.

By the time the first light of dawn creeps through the windows, I give up on getting any real rest. Dressing in casual clothing, I grab a jacket, leave my room and head downstairs, keeping my footsteps light to not wake Sebastian up.

I just need to escape for a little while, to get some fresh air and think.

I don't have a destination in mind. This isn't New York, the place I've lived my whole life. London is literally foreign territory for me. So, I just pick a direction at random and start walking. The sun is rising, so there's little traffic and almost no people on the street. My mind is still a jumble of thoughts about what I did last night, and I don't pay much attention to my surroundings until I spot a pretty park up ahead. It's big and lush, with flowers planted, and walking paths winding through the trees: The perfect place to wander as I try to come to terms with what happened last night.

No, I correct myself. It didn't just happen. Even though he took control—in a way I hate to admit still thrills me—I have to take responsibility for what *I did* last night.

With Sebastian.

Beneath him. Against him. Moaning for more.

My cheeks burn in humiliation. How could I have enjoyed that man touching me? I hate him. I burn to see him suffer, to watch him broken, the way he must have broken Miles.

But still...

I came for him. Willingly. And god, I'd do it all over again.

So what the hell do I do now?

I walk, turning it over in my mind. A part of me wants to just keep on walking: cut and run, and never look back. Sebastian wouldn't know where to find me, everything I've told him is a lie. I could leave at any moment, and not put myself through this anymore.

But I can't.

I vowed vengeance, and I won't back down. Miles deserves some form of justice, and I'm going to be the one to give it to him. That means using whatever is in my arsenal against the man that manipulated him.

My body can be a weapon. I'm using it to lull him into a false sense of security.

Yes, it's hard to forgive myself for enjoying it, but I just have to reframe how I look at that. I'm using him. I'm getting close to him and if that means taking my pleasure at the same time...

Well, why not? After all, Sebastian wouldn't hesitate to take everything he wanted. Anything. He wouldn't feel an ounce of guilt or remorse about doing whatever it takes to destroy his enemy.

So why can't I? I still loathe the man. I'm not wavering in my determination to hurt him. If anything, the guilt I feel over my pleasure only fuels me even more.

Besides, even I'm not naïve enough to think that this sexual draw between us isn't helping me get closer. Sebastian clearly loves the idea of teaching me the ways of seduction, being the first man to know my body like this. If I can keep him focused on his conquest, then maybe it'll distract him, provide me an opening to have my revenge.

Reassured, I start walking again, slower this time. I stroll out of the park and down the road. I don't remember which direction I came from in my frazzled state, but I don't really care right now. I'm not ready to go back to Seb yet. I'm enjoying this chance to clear my mind.

I spot a coffee shop and head in that direction. There's a long line, but I'm not in a hurry, but when I'm finally placing my order, I realize that I recognize a woman at a table nearby. It's the blonde from the club bathroom last night, the one asking all those casual questions about Sebastian.

"Lulu?"

She looks up from her laptop and breaks into a delighted smile. "Avery!" she beams. "My sanitary savior."

I laugh. "That has to be the weirdest nickname ever."

"Are you grabbing coffee?" she asks. "The matcha lattes are amazing."

"I'll have to try one next time," I say, "I just kept it plain today."

They call my order, and I go pick it up.

"Here, come take a seat," Lulu says, gesturing to the spare chair.

"Aren't you working? I don't want to interrupt."

"Please, I'm dying for a break," she insists. "It's either you, or browsing the boutiques nearby, and my checking account can't take it. So, stay."

"Well, for the sake of your savings..." I agree, taking a seat with a smile.

Lulu closes her laptop and tucks it into her bag. "What brings you to this part of town?" she asks.

"I was just out for a walk," I say. "Taking a look around."

"Coming from Sebastian's place?"

I pause. "How would you know that?"

She gives a little laugh. "Educated guess, from the way he was looking at you last night. Plus, the houses in this area are pretty pricey," she adds. "Mere mortals like us can only dream, right?"

"Right," I echo with a smile, but my spidey senses are definitely tingling now. "And yes, I'm staying with Sebastian at the moment."

Her eyes widen. "Does that mean you guys are in a real relationship?"

OK, that's enough.

"What is it to you?" I ask, fixing her with a challenging stare. "Why are you asking so many questions about him? And don't lie," I add. "You're not great at it."

Lulu winces. "Shit. I thought I was playing it cool. Okay, fine. I'm a journalist. At least, I want to be," she adds, "but right now the *Gazette* has me stuck on the social diary, writing about charity luncheons and polo matches. I figured, if I could get a story about the great Sebastian Wolfe..."

I frown. "So, you've been following me to try and get some kind of scoop?"

"What? No!" She protests, and this time, I can see it's genuine. "This is a total coincidence, I swear. I couldn't help asking, I didn't mean to lie. Forgive me?"

I think fast. Lulu clearly knows more than I do about London society, and even if she's got her own agenda here, well, so do I.

Maybe we can be useful to each other.

"Forgiven," I reassure her with a smile. "Although, you owe me two drinks, now."

"How about lunch?" she offers immediately.

My phone buzzes in my pocket, and I pull it out. Sebastian's calling. I click to send it to voicemail and tuck it away again.

"You know what? I am hungry." I smile. "Do you know anywhere good to eat?"

"There's a great spot, just around the corner."

"Perfect."

We leave the coffee shop and head to a nearby café. We sit outside, under a candy-striped awning, and order delicious looking meatball sandwiches that Lulu swears are the best in town.

"I don't know," I tease. "A New York sub sets a pretty high bar."

Lulu groans, "I love New York, you're so lucky. Did you grow up there?"

I pause. As much as I want to be her friend, I know that I need to be careful. Lulu is a journalist with an agenda, so I can't be completely honest about who I am. I have to maintain the fabricated identity that Sebastian knows.

"Upstate," I say, keeping it simple. "But I've always wanted to travel, so it's nice to be somewhere different."

"And I'm sure you're experiencing the best of the city with a man like Sebastian Wolfe." Lulu says, sounding envious. "That man has the entire world is at his feet."

"Right?" I agree. "Although, he's kind of an enigma. I'm still trying to figure him out."

"Well, good luck learning anything," Lulu says, clearly happy to gossip. "He's quite the mystery. Lots of journalists want the scoop on him, but the most that anyone knows is that he's got tons of money, a string of women, and a cutthroat reputation in business."

"That's it?" I ask, disappointed. "No one knows anything else about him?"

"If they do, they're not talking." Lulu shrugs. "Not that I can blame them. I wouldn't want to cross a man like him either. He's kind of scary, don't you think?"

"I like a powerful man," I declare, and she giggles.

"Don't get me wrong, I wouldn't kick him out of bed either!"

It's amazing how much of an open book Lulu is, but I'm glad. Even just learning that he's a fiercely private man is helpful. It reenforces my resolve to use my body to get close to him. It might be my only way in.

"How long have you been looking into him?" I ask casually. My phone buzzes in my pocket, but I don't even take it out this time. I'm sure it's Seb again, and I'm not ready to talk to him.

"Oh, I'm not really investigating him, or anything like that," Lulu says. "I'm just curious. Everyone is," she adds. "I mean, he's one of the most powerful men in the finance world. Plus, it's all so tragic, what happened with his father."

I perk up. "What happened?"

"You don't know?" Lulu looks surprised.

"I mean, I know he passed away, when Sebastian was younger." I say quickly.

"It was so sad. Car crash," she says. "He ran the car off the road, straight into a lamppost."

"That's awful," I agree. "Was Sebastian hurt?"

Lulu shakes her head. "He wasn't there."

"Oh. Still, awful," I agree, making a mental note to dig into it more.

"Aside from that, it's just the usual playboy stuff with Seb," Lulu continues. "Yachts, and racetracks, and—" her eyes suddenly bug out of her head, looking at something behind me.

I turn, just as Sebastian saunters over to our table.

What the hell?

He looks angry until he takes in the sight of me sitting with someone else. That makes him change his features to a pleasant smile as he reaches us.

"Avery, darling," he says as he reaches us. "I thought that was you I saw when I drove by. Hi there," he adds, smiling at Lulu.

"Hi," she breathes.

"We were just grabbing some lunch," I say brightly, wondering how on earth he happened to find me.

"Making friends already? How nice." Sebastian gives me a steely gaze, then reaches out his hand. "I'm Sebastian Wolfe."

"Lulu Sharp. Nice to meet you."

They shake hands, and to anyone looking on, it would seem like a perfectly normal interaction, but I know he's studying her, trying to figure out who she is.

"Well, as much as I hate to drag Avery away, we have some-where we need to be," Sebastian continues.

"Really?" I say. "I'm still eating."

"I'll have my chef make you make something at home. Come on."

There's no room for argument. I can see that in his eyes. He's going to drop this charming act any second, which will make things awkward and possibly scare Lulu away from me. I don't want to miss out on an opportunity to learn more from her, so I decide to let him win this one.

"You know what? He's right," I say to Lulu with an apologetic smile. "I forgot that I have somewhere to be. I'll see you soon, I hope?"

"Absolutely! I'll call you."

We exchange numbers, and then I let Sebastian practically drag me back to the car. He slams the door behind us, and we pull away from the car without a word.

He's fuming, I can tell.

But so am I.

We ride back to the house in silence. The elevator ride up from the underground parking garage is full of tension, but I wait until we're inside the house and alone to confront him. By now, my own irritation has escalated, and I can't hold back.

"How did you find me?" I demanded, turning on him as we reach the foyer. He heads to the living room instead of answering, and I follow. I'm not going to let him get away with ignoring me after that scene at the café. "Seriously, you just happened to be driving past one random café in the whole city?"

"I have my ways." Sebastian answers coolly.

I'm struck with a sudden thought. "Did you track my phone?"

He doesn't reply, but I have my answer.

"I can't believe it!" I exclaim. "Who the hell do you think you are?"

"You didn't pick up my calls."

"Because I was busy," I scowl.

"You didn't say where you were going," Sebastian continues, looking pissed. "You left before anyone was up."

"Because I needed some space!" I cry. "I just went for a walk, for God's sake. Or am I supposed to be a prisoner here?"

"You can go anywhere you like," Sebastian says, his jaw clenched. "Just as long as you let me know where you are."

"Why? So you can keep tabs on me?" I know I should dial it back, not make him angry, but I can't help it. I wanted space away from him, and being back in the same room, so close, seeing the pent-up intensity in his gaze...

It's hot.

And I hate myself for thinking that, even for an instant.

"I always keep track of my property, especially the valuable things." Sebastian says, and I give a laugh of disdain. "You don't go anywhere without my knowledge."

"*Property?*" I scoff. "You don't own me. I'm here because I'm choosing to be here, because I don't exactly have ten million in loose change just sitting around to buy my way out of your arrangement with Nero. But don't for a minute think that gives you control over anything more than my time," I add, stabbing my finger towards him. "One month of my presence, that's all you get."

"Then you're mine for the whole month," he says, stepping closer to me with a heated look in his eyes. "That means you don't take off in the early morning hours without me knowing where you are. *And* you answer when I call."

I fold my arms. "What if I don't?"

I know I shouldn't challenge him like this, but I can't help pushing back, and letting part of my real personality show. I've been acting meek and docile for too long, with all those fucking fluttering eyelashes and bashful looks. God, I just want to scream at him, to yell from the rooftops what a cruel, heartless bastard he really is.

"Careful, Sparrow. You don't want to test me." Sebastian glares, taking a step closer to me.

"Don't I?" I taunt him.

"No." He takes another step. His voice drops, low and steely. "Because you might not like what happens next."

"It can't be worse than anything I've endured with you so far," I retort, and then suddenly, I gasp, as Sebastian yanks me into his arms, pinning me back against the wall.

"Endure?" he echoes darkly. He brings my chin up to look at him, his blue eyes cold and knowing. "That's not what it felt like when you were begging me last night, when your body opened up to me, wet and aching. When you came against my tongue, squeezing that tight cunt like you wanted me to fill it all the way up."

A shudder of lust rolls through me at his filthy words.

Fuck.

He's right. I try to fight it, but I can't believe how fast I transition from wanting to strangle him to being flooded with desire.

And it must be written all over my face, because Sebastian gives me a slow, cruel smile.

"That's right, sweetheart. You can try and deny it, but I already know, you love every minute of this."

I shake my head stubbornly, refusing to let him see the truth. "No."

Sebastian glides his other hand over my body, skimming my curves. "You'll do as I say, from now on," he continues, like I haven't even spoken.

"In your dreams."

My voice is weaker. He knows.

Sebastian pauses, his hand grazing casually over my breast. I bite back a gasp, and he palms it again, full and sweet.

Fuck.

I clench my jaw, struggling with the lust he's fueling, hot in my veins.

He smiles, still gripping my chin with his other hand to force me to look at him. "There you go," he croons, satisfied. "You just need the right incentive to behave, that's all."

"I don't want to play your games," I protest, but the way he's rolling my nipple in his expert fingers make my words emerge sounding like a desperate, needy plea.

My body arches closer, betraying me.

"On the contrary," Sebastian replies, still watching me, insufferably smug. "My games are exactly what you need to let go. You don't have to hide it, Avery. This is what you've been waiting for. A real man, to take care of you, and keep you safe. To take care of *everything*..."

His hand moves lower, unbuttoning my jeans, and sliding determinedly beneath my panties.

I draw in a sharp breath as his fingers find my clit, and slip lower, sinking into my wetness.

Still, Sebastian doesn't break the gaze. "Promise you'll always answer when I call you."

I shake my head, even as I arch against his wandering fingers, desperate for their sweet friction.

Sebastian gives it to me, sinking just one finger inside as his thumb brushes my clit in slow, sweet strokes.

"But don't you want to be my good girl?"

An involuntary shudder rolls through me at the words. I clench hard around him, even as I struggle uselessly in his arms to get away.

Sebastian lets out a low chuckle.

"That's right, Sparrow. I know what makes you wet. So, here's how we're going to do this... I'll tell you exactly what you can do to please me, and if you obey, if you're my good girl... You'll get a special reward."

He starts to pump his finger slowly inside me, and *fuck*, my mouth drops open in a silent moan. Sebastian leans in, capturing my mouth in a commanding kiss, plunging his tongue deep in time with his fingers, overwhelming me with sensation until all I can do is whimper and writhe against his hand, barreling closer to the edge, closer—

Sebastian draws away. His fingers still. I make a noise of protest, gasping.

"Why...?"

"I told you; only good girls get a reward." Sebastian looks at me, a harsh edge to his gaze. "So, will you be good for me now?"

Dammit. I want to tell him to go fuck himself. Slap him right across that smug, handsome face. But god, my body is aching, teetering on the edge. I'm close. *So close...*

"Tell me you'll answer my calls." Sebastian commands me again. He flexes again, just once, enough to make me cry out in need.

"Please..." I beg, shaking, hating myself, but needing the release more.

"Say it or this arrangement is over." Sebastian leans in, his lips grazing my temple. "Answer my calls," he demands, his voice shuddering through me, full of steely promise. "Tell me exactly where you are. I'll take care of you, Little Sparrow. I'll give my girl everything she needs."

I wish it was self-preservation that made me finally gasp my assent. That I calculated the risk of Sebastian rejecting me, and calling off this whole deal, and decided it was better to surrender, and cry out 'Yes,' than risk losing my chance for revenge.

But I'm too far gone to care.

I'll take care of you...

The words seem to encircle me, with a seductive power I don't understand. "Please," I moan, begging him. "I'll do what you want. I'll be good for you."

Triumph flashes on his face. "There you go," Sebastian's

fingers slide deep inside me again. "That wasn't so hard now, was it?"

His kiss swallows my sob, harsh and dominant as he shoves me back against the wall, his fingers moving in a frenzy as his mouth claims me for his own. He nips at my lip, painful, as his thumb finds my clit again, rubbing in relentless circles while his fingers plunge inside me, stretching me, sending waves of plea-sure that I can't hold back, I can't stop, I—

Fuck.

I shatter in a sharp burst, pinned there, helpless, to the wall. I'm reeling with the force of it, but Sebastian doesn't even wait a moment, he pulls away, leaving weak-legged and panting.

"Wait..." I gasp, needing to hold onto him—to anything solid, while my world still spins in double-time.

"Our conversation is over. I have work to do." Sebastian licks off his fingers as his eyes flick over me, and the sight of me sagging here, flushed and panting and totally undone, must be pleasing, because he gives an approving nod.

"Now that I know how to make you behave, we shouldn't have this problem again."

With those words, he walks away.

Bastard.

Chapter 11

Avery

Despite feeling like a failure for surrendering to Sebastian's seduction, I finally get a decent night's sleep, and wake feeling more refreshed than I have in ages. I've had enough sleepless nights since Miles died, and my body can't take much more of it.

I need to take care of myself if I'm going to see this through.

I pull on a robe, and head downstairs, bracing myself for whatever Sebastian has planned for us. But when I enter the dining room, I find Leon clearing the table of empty plates, indicating that Seb was already down here and ate breakfast.

"Where is he?" I ask.

"Mr. Wolfe had to go into work early, but he asked me to pass along a message. You're to meet him for lunch at noon with some clients. The driver will be here to collect you."

"OK," I say, knowing that it won't do any good to refuse. Besides, it would just create an opportunity for Seb to try to control me with sexual pleasure, and I don't think I'm ready for another round of that particular game.

Not when my body still shivers for the last one.

"Can I get you some breakfast?" Leon offers politely.

"Just some toast would be great. And coffee," I add with a smile. "Thank you."

He nods, and heads for the kitchen. I wonder what he might know about skeletons in Seb's closet. Of course, I don't think that's an avenue truly worth exploring. After all, Sebastian doesn't strike me as foolish enough to have the man be his house manager if he can't be trusted.

And wealth like Sebastian's buys a whole lot of loyalty.

No, I'll need to look further afield to find anyone with a grudge against him. I'm guessing there are plenty of people who would love to see Sebastian burn—I just have to get my shit together and figure out his weak spots, the way he's already pinpointed one of mine.

Every inch of my traitorous body tingles as I remember the feeling of his hand between my legs.

I shake the thought away as Leon brings my breakfast. "Thanks," I say brightly. He gives me a nod, and retreats.

Well, at least I have some peace and quiet, until lunch, anyway. I finish up my breakfast, and then head back upstairs to test out the gym set-up in my room. I set the treadmill to run at a punishing pace, getting in a good workout as I think over my plans.

Lunch is a good sign. Sebastian is bringing me to meet clients, which means he wants to show me off—or have me see him in his element as the power broker. Another step closer, gaining access to his life. I'll have to make sure I'm an asset, so I can see more of his work and corporate world. Wolfe Capital is his pride and joy, after all—the reason he can wield so much power.

Which makes it a perfect target for me.

What else? Lulu could be a great ally, I decide, pushing my pace faster on the treadmill. She's in the media, curious, and has ambitions of her own. Plus, she's actually fun to be around.

Fun. I give a hollow laugh, trying to remember the last time I had any. Things have been crazy in my life for a long time, even since before I learned about Miles. Nero's been battling rival gangs all year, and only recently came to a détente—thanks to his new wife, Lily. So, my stress levels were already through the roof, even before...

Before I found the love of my life, hanging from a beam in his apartment.

I finally stop the treadmill, panting hard. My heart is pounding, but in a good way. I feel focused, and clear in my task, and ready to take on my enemy.

Even if he doesn't know it yet.

After my workout, I shower and dress, taking my time to select a demure, pretty outfit and blow-dry my hair into a sleek, wavy style. Last night's show of temper might have slid by under Sebastian's radar, but I know, I can't keep fighting with him, pushing back against his arrogance.

No, I need to be the innocent again, so he'll underestimate me.

I pick out a cream colored tweed dress with a matching jacket, and patent leather pumps. I keep my make up light and natural: just some pink blush, mascara, and lip gloss. I'm starting to get used to this look on me. I no longer see a stranger when I look in the mirror.

I'm not sure what to make of that. It's as if this experience is already changing me in ways I never anticipated.

The driver is waiting and whisks me through London without a word. He drops me off at a stylish restaurant, done up in a Scandinavian look, all bleached wood and airy windows. It's no surprise when I find Sebastian sitting at the best table in the place.

And he's not alone.

He's sitting beside an older man with salt and pepper hair and laugh lines around his eyes. There's a woman of around the same age at the table as well, and they all are in the middle of a conversation as I approach.

"Avery, I'm glad you could make it," Seb says when he sees me, all smiles as he stands and pulls me into a warm hug. I blink in surprise, thrown by his friendly attitude.

Sebastian, warm?

He pulls of the empty chair beside him for me, and I sit, my mind racing. "This is Alistair Dunleavey and his wife, Emma," he continues, introducing his lunch guests.

"Nice to meet you," Alistair says, with a Northern brogue to his accent. Up close, he has weathered skin, and a plain cashmere sweater on, and right away I like his down-to-earth vibe. "Seb tells us you're visiting him from the States?"

"Umm, yes," I say, still caught off-guard by meeting someone so friendly. That's not exactly something I've experienced with Sebastian or his associates. "Just for a few weeks."

"Although, I'm trying to convince her to stay longer, isn't that right, darling?" Sebastian gives me a smile and brings my hand to his lips to kiss my knuckles.

And there it is. He wants to play the loving, attentive partner to impress these nice people. Probably, because they'd run for the hills if they knew what a heartless bastard he was.

Oh, this is going to be fun.

I smile back at him, batting my eyelashes. "You'll just have to convince me harder, Pumpkin," I coo, enjoying the way he clenches his jaw at the nickname. I give the others a grin. "Seb is so diligent, I'm sure he'll think of something."

Alistair chuckles.

"Well, I hope you're enjoying your visit to London," Emma adds, looking delighted. "I'm from Wales myself, but I've lived here for the past twenty-five years."

"I'm loving it," I exclaim. "And Seb has been the best tour guide. He's taken me everywhere, even up on one of those double-decker busses to go around town, with a big 'I heart London' sweatshirt on. He lost a bet," I add with a wink.

Alistair blinks. "I can't imagine that," he says slowly.

"I know! He's just the best. And you're in business together?" I ask casually.

Alistair pauses. "I wouldn't say that."

"Not yet, anyway," Sebastian jumps in, still all charm. "I'm trying to talk him into it," he explains to me. "Alistair owns a large shipping company, and I'm determined to invest."

"Well, I can tell you one thing about my Seb," I coo, patting Sebastian's hand. "He always gets what he wants."

"We'll see..." Alistair says vaguely, exchanging a look with his wife. "But enough about business, let's order."

"Great!" I exclaim and open my menu. "Oh look, they have pumpkin ravioli. Pumpkin with my Pumpkin." I grin at Sebastian, enjoying this, and his lips twitch with annoyance—or amusement, I can't really tell.

Either way, I chatter happily to Emma and Alistair as our food arrives, until Sebastian casually steers the conversation back to his planned acquisition, as Alistair talks about his love of fishing.

"Of course, you'd have more time to enjoy the river if you took on partners," Sebastian says smoothly.

"I know," Alistair gives a rueful sigh. "And believe me, I've thought about it. You make a very generous offer."

"So what are your concerns?" he asks.

"It's a *family* company," Alistair says simply. "And it's important to me that it stays that way."

"I understand that." Sebastian says immediately. "Trust me, I get the importance of family legacy. My own father started Wolfe Capital, and that's part of what drives me to work so hard. I'm honoring the blood, sweat, and tears that he put into the business. But we have to think about the future too. Not just the legacy we inherited, but the one we'll leave, too, for our own children. Your company has a brighter future if you get into business with me, allowing your children and your children's children to benefit from the foundations you've set, for years to come."

I blink, impressed. This is a side of Sebastian that I haven't seen yet for myself. Charming. Warm. Sincere.

It would be nice... If a word of it was true.

But still, I can see that our guests are buying it. Emma likes what she's hearing. She doesn't have much of a poker face. But Alistair is still on the fence.

"I'm not trying to give you the runaround," he tells Sebastian apologetically. "You understand that this is a big decision for me. I need to think it over."

"Of course you do." Sebastian says warmly. "Take all the time you need. I wouldn't expect you to commit right this moment. Now, tell me about your children. Greg just got married, right?"

The rest of the business lunch goes by with easy conversation between the four of us. Seb takes any opportunity he can to insert something about how important it is to do honest business and that he looks forward to meeting Alistair's son since he's so sure they'll be in business together. I can tell that he's giving it all when it comes to landing this deal.

But the act only lasts so long. The minute we leave the restaurant, and Alistair and Emma drive away in a cab, Sebastian's warm smile turns to a look of derision.

"What a fool. He thinks he can save his relic of a company."

He pulls out his phone and types out a text message with furious intensity as we get into his car.

"Head to Wolfe Capital," he orders, then sees me watching him. "What?"

"Quite a show you put on in there." I'm careful to keep my voice even.

"You too." He gives me an approving nod. "You did well. Aside from the baby-name business, but I suppose it didn't hurt."

"They seemed nice," I protest.

Sebastian snorts with disdain. "He's a relic, holding onto the past. He might have started the company, but that doesn't mean he's equipped to run it now. He's wasting potential—and profits, with his sentimental garbage."

"So, how will you convince him to sell?" I ask, curious.

"I have my ways," Sebastian says, with a smirk. "But either way, Dunleavey Shipping will be mine by the end of the month."

My stomach twists, but what did I expect? Sebastian may have put on the charm today, but he's still a shark. And he'll just keep going for blood.

Until someone stops him.

I'm expecting the driver to drop me at home, but instead, he takes us into London's financial district. My eye is drawn to a skyscraper that sticks out among all the other buildings. It's tall and shaped differently than any other structure I've seen, resembling an elongated egg, and covered in glass panels. It's the most striking example of contemporary architecture that I've ever seen. When we pull up to this building, I'm not

105

surprised that Seb would have his offices here. It draws attention and is imposing, just like him.

"I have to deal with some paperwork," Sebastian says. "You can wait in the car."

"It's OK," I say quickly. "I'd like to see where you work." I give him a sunny smile, and it must work, because he shrugs.

"It's not that exciting, I can warn you."

"I wouldn't say that," I follow him through the busy lobby, all chrome and class, and over to the elevators. "What you do is pretty impressive. I couldn't imagine doing anything like this."

When we step out on the thirtieth floor, I follow behind Sebastian. I know I'm supposed to be scoping the offices, but I'm momentarily distracted by the view. All of London is stretched out around us, and I can see for miles.

"You really get to look at this every day?" I ask him.

Sebastian blinks, like he's never even noticed. "It's fine, I suppose. This way."

Wolfe Capital is buzzing, with serious looking people tapping away on computers and talking on the phone. The décor is much like the house on the island: all minimal chic, with white and statement modern art.

If a place could smell like money, this would be the scent.

I follow him through the floor, trying to memorize faces as we pass. "You can wait in my office," he says, showing me to a spacious corner room, decorated with nothing but a massive glass desk, executive chair, and then a small seating area.

Talk about a power view.

"I won't be long," he says, closing the door behind him. Immediately, I look around, ready to investigate.

There's not much here to look at. It'd be nice if there was a folder marked 'Sebastian's Dirty Secrets', but I can't even see a laptop anywhere. There's nothing personal to his décor here. No pictures or knickknacks. This could be anyone's office.

Is that a way to protect himself? Or is he so soulless that he doesn't need anything other than the money he makes at this place?

I scan the room. No files, no folders, no desk drawers to rifle through.

Damn it.

I look around the room again, and this time, I notice something uneven about the black marble paneling on one wall.

I move closer and run my fingers over the grooves. I press down, and the panel springs out slightly. I pull and find there's shelving behind it: Bookcases and crevices built into the wall.

The whole place is a filing cabinet!

There's nothing interesting behind this one, just a wet bar with expensive liquor, so I glance quickly at the door to check nobody's coming, before testing another panel.

This one reveals a safe, hidden behind the paneling.

Now we're getting somewhere. I try to pull it open, but it's locked with an old-fashioned lock. I'm immediately intrigued. This is the first thing I've found that's protected. Which means Sebastian feels it's important enough to have a safety measure.

Would he hide the key in here, too?

I won't know for sure unless I look. I go back to his desk, and run my hands over the smooth glass, in case there's some kind of hidden compartment, I search my mind for other options. Inside one of the other panels? Tucked into a secret box?

My eyes land on one of the paintings. Could a key be behind it, hiding in plain sight?

It's worth a shot. I glance at the door, nervous, as I reach for the painting. I carefully pull it out from the wall, peeking behind it—

"Avery?"

I jump, nearly ripping the painting right off the wall in my surprise. I whip my head around to see that Becca has appeared out of nowhere, standing in the now-open doorway.

"Oh. Hi!" I'm trying to sound casual, even as I careful put the painting back into place and wait for my heart to stop skittering in my chest.

"What are you doing?" she asks, frowning. She's wearing another chic business outfit: a boxy navy top with white wide-legged pants, with a flashy gold buckled belt around her waist.

"Just waiting for Sebastian." I say quickly. "He had some papers to sign?"

Becca looks at the painting pointedly.

"It's so pretty, isn't it?" I beam, stroking over the surface like that's what I was doing here all this time.

"Yes, it is," Becca says coolly. "Very delicate too."

"I hope I didn't damage it," I say, acting concerned. "I was just curious about the artist. I didn't see a signature on the front, so I thought I'd check the back."

Glancing at the painting as I speak, I can clearly see the signature there in the corner, but it's the best explanation I can come up with. I'm just glad that she didn't see me snooping through the wall panels. That would have been a tiny bit harder to explain.

"I love your belt!" I blurt, trying to change the subject. "Where did you get it? It's so striking."

"It's Gucci," Becca replies. She's glancing around, like she's trying to figure me out, so I paste on my brightest, most innocent smile.

"Oh, amazing. The shopping here in London is supposed to be incredible. Maybe you can recommend some places for me to check out."

"I don't have much time for shopping," she says, more than a little condescending. "I have a stylist pick things out for me."

"Right, girlboss, I get it." I beam.

"Well, some of us have to work for what we want," she says, her eyes sweeping over me again. "I've worked hard to make it into this office. Nobody held the door open for me."

Ouch. Clearly, Becca thinks I'm just another pampered trophy spending Sebastian's black credit card. Which, to be fair, I am. But I notice how she delivers her comments with a friendly smile, never risking offending the boss's girlfriend.

Smart woman, I think. She'd be surprised to learn we have a lot in common.

Sebastian enters—and then looks surprised, as if he's already forgotten I was here. "All set?" I ask him. "Becca here has just been talking fashion with me, isn't that right?"

Becca manages a smile. "Did the Sullivan files get to you?" she asks Sebastian, already ignoring me.

He nods, dragging a hand through his hair. "They're a mess, and the draft contracts aren't much better. I've called them all in, and I'll personally be going point-by-point until they get it right this time."

His gaze flicks over to me. "You should head back to the house. I'll be here for the rest of the day."

I try to hide my relief. "OK," I say pleasantly, instead. "The weather's so nice, I think I'll take another walk, get to know the city a little." Then, with superhuman control, I add: "I'll call to check in later, let you know where I'm heading."

Sebastian looks surprised—and pleased that I'm agreeing to his demands. "That sounds fine," he agrees, strolling over. He kisses me on the cheek, and then murmurs in my ear. "That wasn't so hard now, was it?"

I want to slap the smug look off his face, but instead, I just smile. "See you later. Bye Becca," I add, turning to leave. She's still looking at me like she's trying to solve a puzzle, and I make another mental note to be careful around her.

She could be trouble for me.

. . .

I leave the office, taking a meandering route towards the Thames, and soaking in the city around me. The sleek office buildings give way to more historic streets, until I find a River-walk path, which gives me a view of all the tourist sites: London Bridge, Big Ben, the London Eye... There are tons of people out, snapping photos, and hustling on their way to work. With so much to see and do, I find myself wishing I wasn't alone.

I've been walking for an hour, when I spot a kiosk selling newspapers and magazines. They also have a few electronics, and I buy a burner phone with cash. It's been too long since I checked in with Nero, and I know I can't risk calling from the cellphone Sebastian gave me.

If he can track it, I'm guessing he can log my calls and texts, too.

It takes a little time to set the thing up, but when I do, I find a spot overlooking the water and dial Nero's number. He answers on the first ring.

"Barretti."

"It's me." I exhale, just hearing a familiar voice. A voice sounding like home.

"Fuck, Avery. I haven't heard from you in damn near a week."

"It's not easy to get away to make a call. Sebastian is always watching."

Even now, I glance around, making sure nobody can hear me.

"Has he hurt you?" Nero demands.

"No, it's not like that," I reply. "You know I can handle myself."

Nero sighs. "I've been worried. Lily is, too."

"I'm fine, really." I lie. "I just need more time. The guy is secretive and paranoid, it's going to take me a while to figure out his weak points."

"Well, if you want ideas of where to start, a man like Sebastian always has enemies," Nero mutters darkly. "They'll be your friends."

I think of Sebastian's uncle, and the weird vibe there when we ran into them. "I'm working on it. I met a woman, a journalist, I might be able to use her to get more information."

"I still don't like this, you know," Nero says quietly. "You're in danger near that man, whether you know it or not."

"I don't care," I tell him, honest. "I have to do this. For Miles."

Nero pauses for a long moment.

"You know that old proverb, right? If you go looking for revenge, you should dig two graves."

I shiver. "The ruthless Nero Barretti is warning *me* about revenge?" I reply lightly.

"You know what I mean."

"I do." I sigh, feeling a pang. "Don't worry, I'll be careful."

We end the call, and I try to decide if it's worth sneaking the phone back into Sebastian's house. I decide against it, and throw the burner in the trash. For all I know, Leon is rifling through my drawers every day, and I can't risk Sebastian seeing I'm still in contact with Nero.

I keep walking, trying not to let Nero's words unsettle me. I knew what I was signing up for, embarking on this mission. I knew how high the cost might be.

But avenging Miles' death is worth it. I'd pay whatever it takes, even if it can never bring him back to me.

I find myself near an outdoor market area, with used books set up on carts, outside the British Film Institute. I pause and browse the books for a moment, before stepping inside to grab a drink in the cafe. There's a classic movie festival going on, and one of the posters catches my eye. *The Godfather Part II.*.

I stop and stare at the poster, an ache slicing through my chest. I've seen the movie. I watched the whole series with Miles, years ago, during one weekend marathon. He couldn't believe I'd never seen them, especially given our line of work. So, he insisted: Ordering in pizza, getting beers, setting up his apartment with a projector and laptop, the whole nine yards.

I spent the whole time sat on the couch beside him, wishing he would reach over and hold my hand, but still, I had the best time. Miles was like that: thoughtful, kind, and sweet. He cared about the people in his life, was fiercely loyal to us—to me, Nero, all the other guys in the organization. He could have done anything with his life, he was smart enough, a real nerd, something. After Nero paid for him to go to law school, he told Miles that if he wanted out of the Barretti organization, he could go. Start over, a blank slate. Go legit.

But Miles stayed. For Nero. And for me, I like to think. He wouldn't go and leave us behind. He was always the angel on Nero's shoulder, counselling him from crossing the line. Trying to protect all of us.

But we couldn't protect him, in the end.

I couldn't.

This is why I'm here. Sebastian shouldn't be walking around happily when a man like Miles is in the ground.

I make a vow to myself right then. I will be ruthless to avenge him. No matter what it costs me.

Chapter 12

Sebastian

Nine-to-five doesn't apply when you're running a billion-dollar empire. I do what needs to be done, regardless of the time of day or day of the week—and I expect my team to do the same. I've burned through three assistants in the last year because of it, but I have no plans to change my ways.

That's why I'm at the office late into the evening. I'm in the conference room with a select team whose main goal is to obtain Alistair Dunleavey's shipping company. Whatever it takes.

"Dunleavey is still on the fence," I inform them, annoyed. "Which means we need to prep for two scenarios: a willing partnership, and a hostile takeover."

Of course, even the partnership option wouldn't let Alistair keep control for long. I'd have him out the door in a week, thanks to my cutthroat legal team. But he doesn't know that.

One of my new researchers looks uneasy. "I'm not sure... If you want to proceed in a more aggressive manner, we need to talk to legal about our options."

"Legal will just have to find a way," I snap, irritated. "I don't want to hear reasons why I can't do something. I want solutions. Fast. And if you want a future at Wolfe Capital, you'll learn to never tell me 'No' again," I add.

The guy quakes.

"Anything else?" I look around, impatient. There's no reply. "Good, that means you'll have a plan for me by the end of the week."

I walk out, back to my office. Becca joins me there, a moment later. "Nice inspirational speech there, coach," she quips. "Clear eyes, full hearts."

"Is that some TV reference?"

"Forget it," she says, clearly sensing I'm not in the mood for chitchat. That's one of the things I can depend on with Becca: She doesn't waste time on petty bullshit. Not when there's money to be made. "I'll convene with legal tonight, start drawing up plans."

I nod, pleased. It's already past nine p.m., but don't tell her it can wait until morning, or for her not to interrupt her plans. I pay people for their time, and absolute dedication. "And fire the new kid, whatshisname."

"Kenny," Becca sighs. "I could use him on this, his research has been excellent."

"Fine. Have him complete the project, *then* fire him," I agree. "He's clearly not cut out for the place."

She nods in agreement. I head for the door, but Becca lingers, and I can see there's something she wants to say. "More thoughts on the takeover?" I ask.

She shakes her head. "Avery seems sweet," she says instead.

I stop. "You've never been one not to speak your mind," I point out dryly. "Why start now?"

Becca looks amused. "Fair enough. I don't trust her."

I wait, surprised.

"I don't know how you met, or what you think her deal is, but the girl has an agenda," Becca continues.

"What makes you say that?" I ask, curious. Becca has great instincts—usually.

"No reason I can put my finger on," Becca shrugs. "Just a gut reaction."

"Well, this time your gut might be mistaken," I reply. I'm the one who masterminded Avery's entry into my life, she was just a pawn in a bigger game. "Really," I add, seeing Becca's genuine concern. "She's young and naïve, and her only agenda is to get under my skin and piss me off whenever she can."

Becca looks wary, but gives a shrug. "Whatever you say, boss. But watch out. Sometimes, the most innocent ones have the sharpest edge."

I head home, but Becca's words linger in my mind.

Could Avery be hiding something from me? My own instincts wondered if she was holding something back, but I figured it was just her sexual inexperience, and how thrown she is by her burgeoning desire.

And fuck, that desire is intoxicating.

It's a new kind of rush, watching her discover what it means to want somebody. To need *me*, even though she tries her best to fight the desire.

But I will always win. And now I know her weaknesses... The way her slick cunt gripped around me when I told her she was a good girl. That flash of lust and shame when she finally broke down and begged me for more.

She wants to be controlled. Dominated. To follow my instructions and seek my praise as a reward.

Fuck, I'm hard just thinking about it. The things I'm going to teach that girl...

The ways I can corrupt her innocence.

She's awakened a possessiveness inside of me that's beyond anything I've ever experienced before. When I found her gone from the house, and she didn't answer my calls, I thought she'd left me.

The fury that consumed me. The fear, too, when I wondered if something had happened to her... If someone had *taken* her.

I need her to belong to me. Completely.

But why?

It's not just her innocence. I've never cared about that shit before. No, my lust for Avery is primal. Some elemental part of me demanding that I claim her as my own, as if there's something inside her that I recognize.

So maybe Becca is right, and Avery is hiding more than meets the eye. Maybe that's what's calling to me.

After all, I know plenty about darkness and secrets. About hiding your true, twisted nature in plain sight.

I know what it is to masquerade as a regular person, knowing there's nothing redeemable in your heart.

I text Leon to dismiss the staff before I get home, and I arrive to find the house empty and dark. I head to my office and pour a glass of the best scotch in the house. I take a long sip, exhaling. I'm wound tight, but it's not the long day at work that's making me so tense.

It's anticipation.

Now, it's time for Avery's next lesson.

I hear music faintly playing, some radio station I guess, and I follow the music to the family room, where Avery is playing an old vinyl record from my collection, singing along in perfect tune.

Her voice shivers in the air. Angelic.

My runs hotter as I watch her sing the haunting melody.

Her eyes are closed, and she's lost herself in the music, totally absorbed.

The way she looks when I'm pushing her to the brink of pleasure, about to climax.

Her eyes open suddenly, and she stops suddenly when she sees me.

"Sorry," she blurts. "I didn't know you were back."

"Don't stop," I tell her, moving closer.

But she shakes her head. "It's fine, I was just messing around. Did you get everything settled at the office?"

She looks up at me, her eyes wide and curious. For a moment, I'm tempted to just collapse on that pristine couch I never use, telling her about my day. Pour another drink for her so we can talk for a while. Pull her into my lap and feel that delicious body pressed against me. Relax, just for a moment.

But as soon as the thought enters my mind, I push it back. Sitting. Talking? The idea is unthinkable.

Who the hell do you think you are?

Men like me don't get the luxury of letting our guard down, not even for a minute. My control has always been my strongest weapon, and there's no way I can let it slip, not even for this girl with the voice of an angel, and body that could tempt any virtuous man to sin.

But I'm not virtuous. Not even close. And I need to show Avery, I'm not here for chitchat and cuddles.

"We're going out," I say instead of answering her question.

"It's late," Avery gives me a sleepy smile. "Couldn't we just stay in, relax? I want to hear about your day."

The temptation I feel to do just that is proof that I need to change things up.

This is my world. My terms. And I think we both need a reminder just how true that is.

I feel a surge of determination. I know exactly what tonight's lesson will be. One she'll never forget.

"Go get dressed," I order her coolly. "Something that shows you're mine."

It might be late, but the night is just beginning.

Chapter 13

Avery

Sebastian wants something, I can tell from the determined glint in his eyes. I'm learning to read his signals now, and everything about him is on edge, like he has something to prove.

Whatever it is, I can take it.

I hope he liked the show, back at the house. Of course I knew he was home, I was waiting in the living room, until I heard his footsteps, and started my performance for him.

He likes his Little Sparrow blushing and innocent?

I can play that game as long as it takes. Wearing whatever costume he likes.

I quickly select a little black dress to wear for him tonight, figuring that I can't go wrong with that. I bought a few pricey pieces of jewelry when I went shopping a few days ago, and I'm wearing diamond earrings, too. Strappy black heels complete the look, and I pin the flowing waves of my hair back off my neck.

When I come back down the stairs, Sebastian is already waiting for me. His eyes start at my feet as I'm coming down the stairs and work their way up. The intensity of his stare is almost like a physical caress, and I feel a shiver slide down my spine.

Yes, he's on a mission tonight.

Just like me.

"The driver's outside. Let's go." He opens the front door for me.

"Where are we going?"

He doesn't reply. Of course not. But I don't argue. I sit silently beside him in the car as the driver whisks us through the lights of London, until we arrive in a neighborhood full of huge stucco mansions. The car pulls through a pair of gates, and up a driveway to the house.

I can hear music as we get out of the car, a thumping bass that ripples through the night.

Sebastian leads me into the party, and I'm immediately overwhelmed by all the people and the volume of the music. Everyone looks young and glamorous, wearing glittering designer outfits. There are people dancing in every room, food and liquor flowing... a real wild party. We've barely made it five feet through the door before I spot a man doing a line of coke off the swell of a woman's huge breasts in her low-cut dress. I recoil, moving closer to Sebastian.

He gives me a long look. "What's wrong, Sparrow? Worried you might see something you'll enjoy?"

Before I can reply, a man strolls towards us down the hallway. He's tall and dark-haired, wearing all black and three-day stubble on his smirking, handsome face. He slows as he approaches us, looking me over with clear appraisal.

"Wolfe," the man greets Sebastian with a smile. He's English too, with a cut-glass accent that makes me think of aristocracy. "Gracing us with your presence, what an honor."

"Saint." Sebastian chuckles. "I like to show you all what you're missing, from time to time."

"Arrogant tosser," the man says good-naturedly. Then the men hug, slapping each other on the back in a friendly, familiar gesture.

I blink, shocked at Sebastian's easy banter and genuine show of warmth.

The big, bad wolf has real friends? Named... Saint?

Saint's gaze drifts over to me. "And who is this charming lady?"

"Avery," he replies.

"Charmed." Saint takes the hand I offer and brings it to his lips in a playful kiss.

"Did you say your name was Saint?" I repeat, not sure if I heard that right.

"Anthony St. Clair, at your service, but I go by Saint. That's the name the women scream in bed, at least," Saint says with a wink. "You can ask Seb all about that."

I look at Seb curiously.

"We went to university together." His words don't really explain anything, and the pair of them share a look that speaks volumes. There's something I'm missing here.

Sebastian looks between us and gives a cryptic smile. "I'll go get us some drinks," he says, and then disappears into the crowd.

Saint steers me to a quieter room in the back of the house, with large couches strewn about. "So you've known Sebastian a long time?" I ask, not wanting to waste this opportunity to dig for info with someone who has history with him.

Saint settles beside me. "Unfortunately," he grins. "We met back at Oxford."

"What was he like back then?" I ask eagerly.

"Oh, the same arrogant control freak," Saint replies. "But enough about him, I'm more curious about you."

He drapes an arm over the back of the couch behind me, his fingertips grazing my bare shoulder.

I pause. Is this man being friendly, or...?

"I'm not that interesting," I reply with a shrug.

Saint chuckles, his gaze running up and down my body. He doesn't even try to hide the fact that he's checking me out. "I sincerely doubt that. How long has Sebastian been hiding you away from us?"

"Not long," I reply. "I don't really know him that well yet."

"What's there to know?" Saint says. "As long as he's taking good care of you." He pauses, his fingertips brushing me again. "Is he?"

I flush. There's something about the amusement in Saint's eyes that makes me wonder what's going on here. If he knows Sebastian—if they're friends—he would never just go around hitting on his girl, not after seeing how possessive Sebastian is. It's a recipe for disaster—and total self-destruction.

So what's the game here?

"I'm just curious about him," I say, deciding it's best to play along. "What was he like when you met him?"

"Seb back in the day?" Saint smirks. "He was pretty much the same as he is now. Intense. Lord and master of all he surveys."

"And you're not like that?" I ask, adding a flirty note.

"Well, I can tell you a secret," he says, moving to fully rest his arm around my shoulders. He leans in, breath hot against my cheek. "Sebastian's the sinner, and me? I'm the saint."

He caresses me again. I freeze, unsure of what to do.

Then, I see Sebastian return, walking toward us with drinks in his hand.

Fuck.

I recoil from Saint, expecting Sebastian to cause a jealous scene like he did with the handsy jerk at the club, but he doesn't even flinch.

"I see you two are getting along," he says instead, with another cryptic smile.

"Just like old times," Saint says, taking a glass from Sebastian and raising it in a toast.

"Perhaps the three of us should get together for dinner sometime."

"Perhaps," Sebastian agrees, giving me an appraising look. "What do you think, Avery?"

"Sure, why not?" I blurt. Clearly something here is going way over my head. I bounce up. "Bathroom?" I ask.

Sebastian nods down a hallway. "That way. Don't get lost."

"And if you do, have fun!" Saint adds with a wink.

I leave the room and make my way through the crowd, glad to have a moment to breathe. This party is like nothing I've seen before. It's elegant and sophisticated sure, but it has a wild, end-of-the-world feel too: People doing lines of coke off priceless antiques, right beside a table of people playing serious games of chess—in their lingerie. And in the corner... I see a couple, writhing together.

And they're not just dancing.

I need a moment to catch my breath, that's for sure. And watching all this blatant debauchery... My body is getting hotter, *tighter*.

Like there's sex in the air.

I climb the grand staircase to get away from the crowd and find a bathroom. But I'm just finishing up, when I hear two women enter the boudoir area, just outside.

"I don't know who she is," one of the women is saying. "But it hardly matters. She's obviously just the flavor of the month."

"Yeah, and I don't know why he's parading her around

anyway," the other woman adds. She has an American accent. "She's not Wolfe's usual type."

Sebastian. They're talking about me.

"Seems timid to me. I doubt she's giving a man like him what he needs in the bedroom."

"You know men like Seb, they're all about conquest. That whole virginal thing."

"Right," they giggle. "He'll be bored with her in a month."

"Try a week!"

"Or the instant his dick gets wet."

Their voices fade, and I exit the bathroom, feeling a curious stab of disappointment. I should be happy, I'm clearly selling my sweet and innocent act, but if they're right... If Sebastian loses interest with me the minute I have sex with him...

Then I'll be in trouble.

I drift back out, but I'm not ready to rejoin the party just yet. Instead, I find an open mezzanine area, a balcony over-looking the great room below. From up here, I can watch the pulse and writhe of the bodies dancing beneath me. I feel like I'm getting a glimpse at a completely different world. These people are wealthy and reckless, the kind that admire a man like Sebastian, uncaring of the fact that he's a monster that crushes people just for fun.

Who doesn't think twice before taking anything he wants.

I shiver again, although with desire or fear, I'm not sure. I've never felt more out of place—or in over my head. How am I supposed to keep a grip on my mission with Sebastian, when everything is so new to me?

I thought I knew exactly what I was getting myself in for with this mission. But every day with Sebastian, I'm shown something new. Unexpected.

Tempting.

I hear someone approach behind me, and I startle, whirling.

"Easy, Sparrow." It's Sebastian, but I already knew that. The man could walk into a pitch-black room, and I would still know it's him from the arrogance in his bearing, and that all knowing, all-powerful look in his eyes.

"Enjoying the party?"

"No." I reply. "I wouldn't have figured it for your scene."

He arches an eyebrow. "Why not?"

"Look around," I say, nodding to the mindless debauchery below. "It's all just... Shallow, and reckless. You would never lose your inhibitions like that."

Sebastian smiles at me, slow and deadly. "You're right. I couldn't give a damn about the place."

"So why did we come?" I ask.

"For you."

He moves closer, until I'm pinned between him and the wrought iron balcony. Then he turns my body so I'm facing the party again, his breath hot on the back of my neck. "We came here tonight for your next lesson, my sweet."

I shiver, his arms encircling me, so I'm pressed back against his chest. He casually moves my hair aside and presses a hot kiss to the side of my neck. "Look at them," he orders me softly. "What do you see?"

"People who have too much money, who've never faced a single moment of consequence in their lives," I reply, unable to keep the sharpness from my tone.

Sebastian chuckles in amusement. "Look closer."

I shrug, not sure what he wants from me—and already distracted by the slow caress of his hand, tracing light circles on my stomach through my dress. "I don't know. They don't care about anything."

"Good." Sebastian's voice is low. Hypnotic. His hand drifts up. "They're utterly self-absorbed. They take their pleasure, however they want it."

His hand closes around my breast, squeezing me through the fabric. I gasp. "Seb—" I start, trying to pull away, but he keeps me pinned there, trapped against the balcony.

"What's the matter, Sparrow?" he asks, sounding amused. He pinches and rolls my nipple, and I shudder with the pleasure of the gesture, but still, the lights are all on, and the wrought iron balcony offers no protection at all.

We're in full view of anyone who glances up.

"We can't," I blurt, twisting my head to try and look at him. "People will see."

Sebastian's expression is totally calm. Almost detached. "See what?"

"See you touching me," I gasp again, as he continues palming my breasts, which feel swollen and aching in his hands.

"So what?" Sebastian says, leaning to drop a hot, slow kiss on my neck. "Let them watch."

I shudder. He can't possibly mean...?

But he can. And he does.

As one hand continues squeezing and playing with my breasts through my dress, Sebastian's other hand moves lower. Down my body.

I tense. "Sebastian..."

"Hush. I know you're already wet for me." Sebastian gives me a possessive stroke through my dress, right between my thighs.

I bite back a moan.

"Yes, that's right. Wet and dripping for me. Because it excites you, doesn't it? The thought of me touching you here, in front of everyone..."

I gasp for air, feeling dizzy. Overwhelmed. "No," I reply, but my voice is barely a whisper.

"Yes." Sebastian strokes me again, and I can't help arching

against his hand, needing more. "I see you, Avery. The flush in your cheeks. The tremble in your knees. The way you're already panting, needing me to rub that sweet clit and make the ache go away."

I don't even try to deny it this time, I just sink my head back against his chest, closing my eyes as he slips his hand up under my skirt, and tugs my underwear aside.

I know resistance is futile. The only thing I can do is sink into the pleasure, and try and forget where I am.

But Sebastian stops.

"No," he scolds me, cold. "You don't get to hide. Open your eyes. Spread wider for me. That's right."

In a daze, I do as he says, staring out at the party again as Sebastian's wicked fingers begin to work me, rubbing my clit in swift, sweet circles under my dress, right here for anyone to see.

"Look at you, with your legs spread, so wet and ready for me," Sebastian muses, sounding smug. "My good Little Sparrow. Now everyone can see what a good girl you are."

I shudder with heat—and humiliation.

Oh God, what am I doing?

I grip the balcony railing, my legs weak as Sebastian keeps up his sweet, teasing torment.

"How does it feel, knowing anyone could see you like this?" he demands, his touch growing rougher. He curls a finger up inside me, and then another, and I have to bite back a desperate cry of relief at the thick, filling friction.

"That's right, baby, moan for me."

I clamp my lips together. *No.* I can't make a sound. Nobody's noticed us yet, but if they hear me...

The thought is hot in my veins, somehow making me even more turned on with twisted shame.

"What a pretty picture you make for them," Sebastian keeps up his dark words, hot in my ear. "God, I should sell tickets. You panting here with your skirt hiked up and my fingers buried in your cunt. But you'd love that, wouldn't you? You'll do anything I want, anything to feel what only I can give you."

He pulses thick inside me, palm grinding against my clit, and I can't help the sob of need that sounds from my lips. It's swallowed by the music, but Sebastian hears it, I can tell from the twitch of his erection pressing into my ass.

"Maybe you need something more than my fingers..." he muses, thrusting again, making me sob. "Maybe you should take my cock, right here. With the whole world watching as I claim this virgin pussy. Show them all who's making you moan."

I panic, the fear twisting with my gathering desire in a hot, anxious flood. "Seb," I blurt, writhing against his hand. "No, you can't—"

"I can do anything I want," Sebastian growls. He fucks me with his fingers again, deeper, as his other hand settles around my throat. Squeezing gently, making me gasp for air.

"You're mine, Little Sparrow," he says calmly, even as my body is soaring, cresting, tangled up in sensations I've never felt before. He squeezes my throat again, and I sob, drowning in the pleasure of it, the dark, velvet rush. "If I want to fuck you over this railing while the whole damn room cheers my name, then that's what's going to happen. And you'll take it, every inch, because you know, you were made for it, baby. You were made to serve me. Receive me. Be my good fucking girl."

Yes.

Something in me unlocks, a rush of relief and pleasure that makes me limp in his arms as Sebastian's commanding hands control my body, my breath, driving to me to the brink of oblivion. I'm just a willing passenger in my own body now, totally free, and it's all I can do to hold on to the railing and accept the pleasure cresting higher, higher...

And then I look out into the crowd, and see a face turned up, watching us.

Watching me, just the way Sebastian said. With my legs spread, and his fingers in my wet cunt, as he claims his good little girl for everyone to see.

Oh my god.

Pleasure slams through me, uncontrollable, and I climax with a scream.

Fuck!

It's all-consuming, the rush of ecstasy, drowning me in sensation until I'm left reeling, gasping for air. Sebastian slowly releases me, holding me up while I gasp and shudder with the aftershocks of the most intense orgasm of my life.

"Shh... Easy, sweetheart," He smooths my dress down again, and turns me to face him. I'm still starry-eyed and reeling as he takes in my shocked, disheveled appearance.

The triumph in his eyes is like a bucket of cold water to my face.

He won. I did everything he demanded.

And loved it.

How much further will he push me?

And how much more will I beg for?

"It's time to go home," he says, with a wicked edge in his expression. "The night isn't over yet."

Chapter 14

Avery

My nerves are going haywire during the ride back to Seb's place, and I'm not doing a good job of hiding it. I have a bad habit of picking at my fingernails, and Sebastian doesn't say anything, but I know he notices.

When we get back to the house, I don't know what's going to happen. After everything that's just passed between us, I can't imagine what he might ask from me.

Or what I'll willingly do, surrendering to his dominance and pleasure.

The house is empty when we arrive, and Sebastian wordlessly leads me inside. I'm at silent war with myself. A part of me is desperate to know what he's planning for me, but I can't let myself forget why I'm here in the first place.

This is all part of your plan, I remind myself. Blind him to the truth of your agenda, make him so obsessed that he doesn't notice you plotting his downfall, right underneath his nose.

Sebastian heads straight upstairs, and I follow, wondering if this is it. Is he taking me to bed? But instead, he leads me into my own room, to the luxurious bathroom attached.

"I'm going to draw you a bath," he says, giving me a smoldering look.

I exhale, a little relieved—

'and confused. "Why?" I can't help asking.

"You're tense," he says, with a smile. "I'm going to help you relax."

Yeah, I don't think relaxation is on the cards for me tonight, not while I'm anxiously watching Sebastian's every move, watching for the catch.

But he doesn't seem to mind. He leans over, and turns on the faucets for the enormous, claw-foot tub, testing the water and adding scented oils and bubble bath.

I stand in the doorway, watching him, still on alert.

Sebastian looks over, and I must look like a deer in headlights, because he chuckles. "No more surprises," he says, his voice reassuring. He saunters over to me and gently lifts my dress. "Arms up," he murmurs, and I obey. He tugs the satin over my head, leaving me in just my black panties and heels.

I flush. This is the most naked I've ever been in front of him, and I can feel Sebastian's gaze like a caress, stroking over me from head to toe. My skin pebbles under his admiring gaze, and my stomach twists at the hunger in his expression. "Look at you..." he says, and it almost comes out as a groan.

I reach to cover my breasts, but he catches my hand to stop me.

"You don't need to hide from me." Sebastian lowers my hands to my sides, and dips his head to kiss me, softer than anything I was expecting. "I told you, I'm going to take care of you now."

I shiver, swaying closer.

But he pulls away.

"Get in the water and relax. I'll be back."

The tub is filled with bubbles now, and rose-scented oils steam up the room. I turn off the water and slip out of my panties before stepping into the tub. It's just on the edge of too hot, but I sink into the bubbles with a hiss of satisfaction.

Oh, that feels good.

I've been wound so tight all day, and the water feels incredible against my skin. I lay back, tipping my hair into the water and letting the bubbles mound around me. I take a long, deep breath.

Did Sebastian mean it, when he said there were no more surprises in store for me tonight? He's been so gentle, now we're back at the house, a total one-eighty-degree switch from his harsh commands at the party.

His hand, tight around my throat.

I shiver again, but it's not from the water temperature. No, it's remembering how it felt, with him gently squeezing the breath from my lungs, owning my body completely. I should have been terrified, but instead... It was thrilling. Heightening my sense of being overpowered in his arms; intoxicating me with a whole new level of sensual danger.

Driving me to greater peaks of pleasure.

My thighs clench at the memory, even as I feel a rush of shame for the way I came apart, climaxing so hard for his twisted games. Enduring his sexual advances may be necessary for my plan, but what does it say about me than I'm embracing them so eagerly? Wanting more.

Wanting *him.*

"Relaxed, yet?" Sebastian reappears in the doorway, carrying a bottle of champagne. He dims the lights to a soft, sexy glow, and strolls over.

I smile, bashful even though the bubbles are covering my body from view. "Maybe a little...."

"That's a good start." Sebastian sits casually on the floor beside the bath and takes a drink straight from the champagne bottle. "It's been a long week, for the both of us."

I let out a wry laugh. "You could say that."

A week. Jesus. Has it really been so little time?

Sebastian passes me the bottle, and I take a sip. It's delicious, of course, but why would I expect anything else.

"What?" Sebastian has caught my expression.

"Nothing, I just... Is there anything in your life that isn't top of the line?" I ask, a little teasing. "Literally everything in this house is designer, exclusive, and perfect. This champagne probably cost more than most people's rent."

He chuckles. "It's 1928 Krug, so probably."

"How much?" I ask, taking another swig.

"About twenty thousand per bottle," he says casually, and I almost do a spit take.

"So that sip was... a thousand dollars?" I exclaim in disbelief.

He smiles. "Have another."

I do, drinking down the light bubbles. "So, this is what money tastes like."

"Good, isn't it?" Sebastian takes the bottle back. He looks about as relaxed as I've ever seen him, with his shirt unbuttoned at the collar, and his long limbs sprawled on the floor. But the look in his eyes is still hungry; calculating, especially when I idly stretch my leg, the suds slipping over my bare skin.

I watch him follow the line of my calf, all the way to the tips of my toes as I flex them in the air. I feel a curious sense of power, floating here in the bubbles, with the champagne fizzing in my veins.

He wants me...

"You look happy." Sebastian says, getting to his knees.

I swallow. "I can't remember the last time I was happy," I say quietly, before I can stop myself.

He pauses, meeting my eyes with an unreadable look. "We'll have to work on that."

Sebastian reaches for a bottle of shampoo. He pours a small amount of liquid into his palm, and then tilts my head back, slowly massaging it into my scalp.

I sigh with satisfaction.

He's slow and methodical, washing my hair with surprising gentleness. After all the excitement at the party, and the gulps of champagne, I feel weightless and a little tipsy, so I decide to relax and enjoy the sensation while I can. Sebastian's touch is hypnotic, rinsing my hair, and then moving to stroke over my back and arms with a damp flannel, washing me clean.

After the bath, he helps me out of the tub and uses a towel the size of a blanket to dry me off, lingering over every inch of my naked body. I'm too relaxed to be bashful this time, and Sebastian makes no show of hiding his attention, caressing over my sensitive skin until I'm tight and aching all over again.

I move to press against him, but Sebastian steps back. "I think it's time for another lesson," he says softly, and my eyes flare. He chuckles. "You'll like this one, I promise."

"I like all your lessons," I admit, honestly. "Eventually."

"Good girl."

Will those words ever not spark an electric reaction in me? I don't know, but for now, I feel a telltale rush of heat between my thighs, as Sebastian takes my hand and leads me out into the bedroom—and over to the full-length mirror set against one wall, gilt-edged and antique.

He positions me in front of it, standing behind me so I'm leaning back against his chest. "You want to please me, don't you, Sparrow?"

I stare at our reflections, Sebastian's gaze locked on mine in the mirror.

I give a halting nod, my cheeks already burning. I look so small against his larger frame. He's still clothed, but I'm completely naked, on display.

"You can't give pleasure to anyone else, until you learn to pleasure yourself," he tells me, his hands moving lightly over my shoulders... Down my arms... Over to graze my ribcage, tantalizingly close to my breasts.

I gasp in anticipation, my nipples pebbling in stiff peaks.

He sees it in our reflections, and chuckles. "That's right. See how beautiful your body is? How it craves to be touched. Look how you flush when I do this..." He closes his hands over my breasts, and massages them steadily, bringing my nipples between his fingers in a pinch.

I moan, pressing eagerly against his touch, feeling the heat spiral low in my core.

"How does that feel, Sparrow?" Sebastian asks in my ear, his voice thick with lust. "Does that feel good?"

"Yes," I gasp, watching his hands at work. It's thrillingly erotic, to see him touch me like this. To watch myself, naked and fragile in his hands. "So good."

Sebastian lets out a growl and thrusts a little against me. His cock is a hard ridge against my ass, and I move back instinctively to grind against him, as his hands keep massaging me with their expert touch.

My head tilts back to rest on his shoulder and I start to close my eyes, but Seb gives my nipples a quick tweak, making me gasp and lift my head to meet his eyes in the mirror.

"That's right, watch yourself," he instructs me, heated. "Watch how your body responds. Are you wet?"

I give a halting nod.

"Show me."

He takes my right hand, and he guides it down, between

my legs. He nudges them apart, baring me to the mirror. To my own fascinated eyes.

Sebastian nudges my hand deeper between my thighs, until my fingertips brush my clit.

I whimper.

"Touch yourself," he whispers, urging me on. "Feel what I feel when I touch you, see just how wet you are."

I can't even think of resisting. I want it too much. I stroke myself again, then skim my fingers lower, dipping into my wetness. Sebastian groans. "Show me," he commands, lifting my hand away.

My fingers glisten in the dim light.

Sebastian takes my wrist and guides it up towards his mouth. He licks my fingers, and I shudder at the filthy gesture.

"Your turn," he says, and my eyes widen in surprise. But Sebastian is already guiding my fingers to my mouth. "Lick them clean," he murmurs, pressing them into my mouth.

In a haze of desire, I do it, thrilled by the taste of myself, salty on my tongue.

"Good girl. Now, finish what you started. Touch that pretty pussy for me, get yourself off."

I'm so turned on, I don't need any more instruction. I reach between my thighs again and begin to play: Circling my clit in the steady, deep strokes that I know will get me there, every time. It won't take long, I know, with Sebastian's dark gaze locked on me in the mirror, and his hands moving now to caress and tweak at my breasts, my body is already wound tight and ready to break. Sexual tension is thick in the air, and my own touch sends pleasure shooting all the way from my center to the tips of my fingers and toes. Looking into Sebastian's eyes while I do it is the most erotic thing I've ever experienced, but even as I twist tighter, cresting higher, release stays elusive, just out of reach.

A whimper falls from my lips, and I writhe in his arms, desperate.

"I-I can't..." I sob, pressing back against him.

"What do you need?" Sebastian's voice is thick with satisfaction. "What do you want from me?"

I blush. "Your fingers," I gasp. "Please... Inside."

Sebastian lets out another low groan, thrusting against my ass as he covers my hand with his own, stretching me with first one thick finger, and then the next, pumping them deep as I keep up my own strokes on my clit.

"*Fuck...*" my twisted cry of pleasure echoes in the silent house. "There, just like that. Oh *God!*"

The sensations are so good, and I have to force myself not to close my eyes—but I want to watch this, the sight of his hand and mine working together to drive me wild; our eyes locked in shocking intimacy in the mirror.

"That's right, baby," he groans. "Take what you need. Take it all the way." He thrusts his fingers faster, and I speed up too, matching his pace as my body tightens—

I come with a cry, clutching onto him for balance as the pleasure rips through me. My legs give way, but Sebastian's strong arms hold me up, his eyes still locked on mine as the waves crash through me, the muscles of my abdomen tighten and releasing over and over again, my body shaking in his arms.

Oh my god.

I'm shaken by the intensity of the orgasm, how *connected* we were. I'm still reeling from it all as Sabastian produces a robe, wrapping me up in it, and leading me to the velvet chaise. He sits down, pulling me into his lap, and I gladly collapse there, breathing fast.

He strokes my hair softly, holding me curled against him. "You did so well, my Sparrow," he whispers. "I'm proud of you."

I feel a foreign glow of satisfaction at his praise. But slowly, my senses come back to me, and I realize I'm crushed in his arms, with his cock pressed hard against me. I wriggle against it instinctively, feeling Sebastian's hard muscles tense.

His touch is still slow. Reassuring. But I can hear his breathing turn labored, as if he's anticipating something more to come.

I eye the bed, wondering if he's going to take what he wants from me now. But Sebastian follows my gaze.

"Not yet." He reassures me. "You still have a few more things to learn before I reward you with my cock. But tonight, you've been such a good girl for me..." he tilts my face up to look at him, and the lust glittering in his eyes. "I'll give you a taste, if you want. Would you like that?"

I inhale in a rush, my blood running hotter. Despite the questions in my mind, I find myself nodding.

Sebastian's expression darkens. "Get on your knees," he instructs me.

My pulse kicks. I slide off his lap, and do as he says, kneeling on the plush rug in front of him. He undoes his belt, and then his zipper, shoving his pants down so that his cock springs free, a thick, demanding length.

"Look what you've done to me," he groans, and there's something animalistic in his tone. "Fuck, Sparrow, you make me so hard."

I'm transfixed. He's huge, jutting up between us, and I can hardly imagine how he'll ever fit inside of me. Yet, my core is clenching with need for it.

I reach out and touch him, stroking my thumb from root to tip, where there's already pre-cum beading. "That's it," Sebastian groans. "Get your hand nice and wet. Now, open that pretty mouth for me."

My heart is pounding in my ears now, so loud it drowns

everything out. The world has contracted to just this small, seductive corner: Me here, obedient on my knees, and Sebastian looming there above me, fisting his cock, and guiding it towards my waiting lips.

I lower my head, tentatively licking him, then opening wider, and taking him all the way inside. He's so thick, it's a challenge, but I suck him in as far as he'll go, my hand moving to the base of his cock as I adjust to the meaty intrusion. This is all new to me, but I follow my instincts, doing what feels right as I use my mouth and tongue to explore him, bobbing my head up and down.

"Oh God, just like that," Sebastian groans, and his obvious pleasure sends another thrill through me. "Keep going, you can take it. Open wide for me. That's my good girl."

His praise makes me feel powerful. It's intoxicating, filling my mind with one simple thought. No, not a thought, a *need*:

To please him, whatever it takes.

I don't question it. Just like at the party tonight, I surrender completely to the primal instinct. For just this moment, nothing else matters, and god, it feels so freeing. No past, no grief, no twisted lies; just Sebastian's cock and my willing mouth, and the groans of satisfaction as his hands move to tangle in my hair, urging me on.

"Take it, baby. Deeper. All the fucking way."

His grip tightens, almost painful as he thrusts deeper, down my throat. My eyes sting and I start to gag from the thick invasion, but he pins me in place, not breaking thrusts for a second, relentless and deep. "Breathe, sweetheart. You can do it. That's right," he groans, as I choke, struggling to control it. "You're swallowing my cock so well. Such a perfect girl."

God. I moan against him, sucking and bobbing faster, wet and messy and totally surrendered to his dominant commands. He's thrusting up into my mouth, almost animal, and I'm shaking, slick between my thighs as I take it, every forceful inch, until finally Sebastian tears me off him. He's wild-eyed, in a frenzy as he rips my robe down and explodes, releasing his climax over my chest with a guttural roar.

The hot liquid splashes onto my breasts, dripping over me.

Holy shit. I'm stunned by the animalistic force of his climax —and weak with desire, knowing that I did this.

I made him come undone.

"Fuck, darling, you did so well." Sebastian growls, pulling me into his lap and smearing the cum into my skin. I realize that he's writing his name in his own seed.

Wolfe.

The act is lewd and possessive, and God help me, I want him even more for it.

I squirm a little in his lap, and he gives me a knowing grin.

"You want more, don't you?" I don't answer, hating that it's true. He looks way too satisfied with that knowledge as he tucks himself back into his pants. "Good. Then our lesson is complete."

He stands, setting me down on unsteady legs.

"But, why?" I manage to ask, breathless and dizzy with longing.

"Because from now on, whenever you touch yourself, you'll only ever think of me," Sebastian says, his eyes flashing with victory. "It's *my* hands you long for on your body. *My* mouth, driving you wild. And now it'll be my cock you dream about, craving for it to fill you all the way up."

He claims my lips in a hard, deep kiss; tongue plunging deep, until I'm panting.

A kiss of ownership.

Then he's gone, closing the door behind him, leaving me weak with desire.

And covered in his brand.

Chapter 15

Avery

The bastard is right.

After I get cleaned up, I spend a restless night trying to sleep, before finally giving in to the wired lust in my body and sliding a hand between my legs to ease the tension. Memories of his hands on my body—and his cock in my mouth—bring me to a swift climax, but it's not nearly enough to ease the ache.

I lay in bed in the dark, staring at the ceiling. How does he have this power over me? His sexual thrall is like a tidal wave, decimating all resistance in its path. But even though I'm inexperienced, I know this isn't how it normally works. There's not much to compare to Sebastian, just a few fumbling interactions with boys that never left me satisfied.

I was trying to save myself for Miles.

A wave of shame and sadness washes over me. My heart aches for the life I wanted to share with him. A simple, ordinary life together. I always thought it would be the Barretti organization that stood in the way of our happiness. Miles always hinted that once things were settled with the rival gangs, when it was safe, we could be together.

And now, finally, it is settled. We are safe.

But Miles fell victim to a different enemy.

I swallow back my sadness, feeling my heart harden again. My strange sexual connection with Sebastian won't distract me. It can't. No number of orgasms or sexual prowess can erase his crimes.

I get a few more hours of sleep before morning comes. With renewed determination to unravel Sebastian's secrets, I pick out a nice dress and prepare for the day.

I head downstairs, ready to be all smiles and innocence again. Sebastian may love bringing out my passion at night, but I still have a part to play, and I feel like I'm finally making some headway with him. He's opened the door to a physical connection, and now I need him to open up to me on a deeper level, to give me something I can use against him.

I'm baiting my trap. Soon, I'll crush him.

"No, the July files. Right away, boss is waiting." A strange man in a suit passes me by in the hallway, heading for the dining room. I follow, surprised to see that we have guests. I recognize Becca, looking as business-like as ever, so I can only assume the other people I see are also employees of Wolfe Capital. There are at least a dozen people, and they are rushing back and forth between Sebastian's office and the dining room, where the staff has laid out a full spread of breakfast food.

I guess he's working from home this morning.

There's a lot of noise, chatter and movement, and I glance into Sebastian's office to see that he's behind his desk, taking a work call. I wait until he hangs up, and then enter, smiling brightly.

"Good morning," I say, and his eyes snap to me.

"Avery. Hi." He sounds cold and dismissive, as if I'm looking at a stranger.

Yeah, because he's only warm to you when he wants to get physical. Don't forget what a manipulative bastard he is.

"So, you're working from home today?" I ask.

"We'll be busy all day," he says dismissively, his gaze focusing on the screen. "Talk to Leon, if you need anything."

My smile falters. Another day away from him won't get me closer to my goal.

I notice that he doesn't have anything to eat, so I head to the dining room and fix him a plate of food. There are more people around now, so I weave through a crowd to bring it back to him. When I reach his desk and place the food down, he doesn't even look at me, let alone say thank you.

OK. Clearly, he's in 'heartless corporate' mode now, with no time for basic decency.

I'm heading for the door, when another woman rushes in, a gorgeous, willowy blonde in a silky blouse and tight pencil skirt. "New numbers," she announces, going to present the papers to Sebastian.

"Excellent. Thank you, Keira."

"A couple of things you need to see, here and here..." She leans over him, breasts brushing his shoulder as she points out various things on the page. Sebastian murmurs something I can't hear, and the woman giggles flirtatiously, giving him an open view of her cleavage.

I watch them, wondering if he's fucking any other woman right now. He seems fixed on me, but I need to hold his undivided attention for the plan to work.

I retreat to the kitchen, where it's quieter, and navigate the expensive espresso machine to fix a coffee. I'm trying to figure it out, when Becca materializes. "No, it's this one," she says, yanking a hidden lever.

"Lifesaver!" I declare brightly. "You guys are pretty busy, huh?"

"Every deal gets crazy at the end," she agrees. She has dark shadows under her eyes, even through her makeup.

"And I'm guessing Sebastian wants everything perfect," I give her a smile.

She smiles back. "Always."

"He's demanding like that," I agree, fixing the coffee. "I don't know how you've managed to work with him for so long."

"By knowing exactly where I stand, and what my value is." Becca replies. She looks at me a moment, assessing. "Can I give you some advice?"

"Sure," I smile back. "What is it?"

"I don't know exactly what's going on with you and Seb, but I think it's important you know... You're disposable."

I blink in surprise at her bluntness.

She gives me a fake look of concern. "I just think it's important you know, because you seem to be getting attached. You shouldn't fall in love with Sebastian. Women don't last with him. He's all about the conquest, the acquisition. In his relationships, as well as business."

Becca still has that look of sympathy on her face. I'm not sure what her game is, warning me off, but I keep my expression even.

"Thanks for the heads up," I say to her, "I'll definitely keep it in mind. Now, I probably shouldn't keep you. After all, I'm sure you have a lot to do."

"That's right," Becca agrees. "What are your plans today."

"Oh, you know," I reply, sunny. "Shopping, lunch, maybe the salon. Have fun here!"

I breeze off, intercepting Sebastian. He looks annoyed, but

I lean up and land a kiss on his cheek. "I'll get out of your hair and give that credit card a workout. Good luck today."

And then I get the hell out and leave them to corporate domination.

I have the driver drop me off in the shopping district, as I chat loudly about all the designer stores I'm going to hit. But the minute he's out of sight, I pick up another burner phone and look up directions to the nearest library. It's less than a mile, so I walk there, enjoying a slice of freedom and peace I get from being away from Sebastian's world for just a little while.

When the place comes into view, I realize that this isn't any old library. The old building is made of grey stone with tall pillars and a pair of lion statues on each side of the steps leading to the entrance. Inside, there's an arched ceiling with a skylight that allows the sunshine to come inside and brighten the place up. There are rows and rows of shelves lined with books and a computer room directly ahead. To my right, I see a round desk with a librarian behind it, sorting books. She's an older woman with square glasses perched on the end of her nose.

"Can I help you?" she asks in a soft voice as I approach.

"Yes, I'd like access to your old business journals and archived newspapers?" I ask hopefully. "I'm writing a research paper for university."

The lie comes easily. I've thought about this for days. Nero advised that I get an idea of Sebastian's history and any enemies he might have. I don't want to risk searching for it on the computer at his house, or even my phone just in case he has a way of tracking my activity. I'm going old-school with this.

"We have all that digitally archived," she replies, she says, leading me to a study carrell with a computer. There are other young people around me, probably college students, and nobody pays me any attention as the librarian takes her time setting me up with the information I need, about searching their records for keywords and requesting back issues of newspapers.

"Thanks so much," I tell her, settling in the chair.

When she leaves me alone, I set a timer on my phone. I don't want to be here for too long and arouse suspicions. I figure three hours is probably all I can really get away with.

Where to begin?

I use the keyword search to look up all mentions of Wolfe Capital or the Wolfe family. The archives go back decades, and my jaw drops as I get thousands of results.

I should have known, Sebastian makes headlines.

I click an old profile of his father at random.

Error: 404. Webpage no longer at this address.

I sigh. Clearly, most of these old reports will be defunct, but I'm sure there's something I can use. I try another and find that it's a news report about a business takeover by Wolfe Capital. I'm not sure what will turn out to be relevant, so I pull a notepad out of my purse and start taking notes.

Three hours flies by, and my hand aches from all the writing I've done. I don't know if I've really found anything that can help me, but I figure that there's no such thing as too much information. When the alarm on my burner phone goes off, I tuck everything away in my purse and close out of the archive system. On my way out the door, I thank the librarian and tell her I'll be back.

As I head back to the shopping district, I think hard about Sebastian and what my next move should be. It would be easy to write Becca's oh-so-helpful advice off as jealousy, to get me out of the way, but what she told me is true: Sebastian does love the chase. So, I need to step things up to keep his attention. I'm mulling what I can do, when I pass an expensive looking lingerie store.

I smile. This seems like a good place to start.

"Did you have a good day?" I ask Sebastian over dinner, a lavish spread in the formal dining room.

"Hmm?" He looks up from his phone. Everyone from Wolfe Capital has left, but he's still distracted. He keeps checking his messages and has barely sent a glance my way.

Which doesn't exactly give me much confidence in my whole 'Keep him interested' plan. I'm wearing one of the new sets of lingerie I bought today under my dress, the emerald lace not doing much to contain my breasts, but it's not really made for support anyway. This particular bra and panty set is designed for seduction.

Which doesn't seem to be on the menu, judging by Sebastian's complete indifference to me.

"I asked if your day went alright, the big takeover bid?"

He nods. "We're pulling it together."

"I don't doubt it."

There's a pause. "What about you?" Sebastian finally asks.

"Good," I say, picking at the food left on my plate. "I went shopping."

His damn phone is in his hand again. "Get anything nice?"

He's not listening for my answer. It's just an obligatory question.

"Actually, I did. New lingerie."

I throw the words out casually, and it's hard not to flash a smile as his head finally snaps up.

Now I have his attention.

"Really?" he asks, his eyes roaming over me as if he's trying to see through my clothes to what I'm wearing underneath.

I blush. This is still new to me. I'm not skilled at seduction. But I must be doing a good enough job because he takes the bait, and sits back in his chair with an arrogant, smoldering look.

"Well, since I funded these little purchases, I think that means I deserve a look." Sebastian smiles at me. "To make sure they're worth it."

"They are," I say, flirty. I'm just reaching for my buttons, when Leon comes through the door with a bottle of wine.

"Go," Sebastian says, his eyes still fixed on me. "And tell everyone they have the night off."

Leon disappears back into the kitchen. I know that most of the staff has already left for the day, so it won't take long for the few remaining people to clear out.

Sebastian doesn't wait, though. Standing, he takes my hand and leads me through the house to the living room, closing the doors behind us.

"Show me," he commands, and I feel desire pool, low in my stomach. And nerves. I remind myself that I was fully naked with this man just last night, but this feels different. He undressed me then, but now, *I'm* trying to entice *him*.

I start to undo the buttons on my silk blouse. I'm only on the second one when he speaks again.

"No." Sebastian says, his eyes burning into mine. "*Slowly.*"

He strolls over to the stereo system and scrolls on the screen. A moment later, sultry music plays all around us, drifting from invisible speakers. Sebastian settles in a large wingback chair and waits expectantly.

He wants a show.

I gulp. I've never given a striptease before, but I guess I'm about to learn—and fast.

Slowly, I unbutton the rest of my blouse, letting the music wash over me. There's a heavy beat, one that I can move to, and

I allow my hips to sway from side to side, feeling Sebastian's gaze slide over me. The hunger in his eyes gives me new confidence, and by the time I peel my blouse away and let it fall to the floor, revealing the balconette bra, I'm totally in the moment.

Sebastian isn't looking at his phone anymore, after all.

I kick out of my shoes and unbutton my jeans, then slowly shimmy out of them. Sebastian leans forward, watching intently as I peel them down, inch by inch. The panties I picked out are only a slip of silk, edged with tiny ribbons, and I can tell he likes them.

Still, Sebastian doesn't say anything until I'm standing there, in just the lingerie set. I strike what I hope is a sultry pose. "You like it?" I ask, and then slowly turn in a circle, displaying myself to him.

Sebastian makes a noise of satisfaction. "I do like it. Come here."

I sashay over to him, step by slow, seductive step. When I reach the chair, he pulls me down, so that I'm straddling his lap.

"Very nice..." Sebastian traces the edge of my panties. His leans forward, licking against my nipples through the flimsy fabric of my bra until they're hard and aching. I feel the stiff ridge of his erection pressing into my lap, and I automatically rock against it.

Sebastian sucks in a breath, lifting his head to give me a dark, delicious smile. "You're learning."

I blush.

He unzips his pants, freeing the thick length of his cock between us. "Now, do that again," he instructs me, holding my gaze. "Grind against it."

I do what he says, breathless. There's as erotic thrill from feeling his cock like this, rubbing against my clit with only a thin layer of lace separating us. I let out a moan, rocking against him, loving the pressure.

"That's it, Sparrow." Sebastian grips my hips tightly, bringing me into him. "Take your pleasure from me."

I rock again, grinding, chasing where the friction feels the best. Sebastian's breath quickens, watching me with a fevered look in his eyes, like he's holding back, keeping control.

He takes my hand and brings it to my mouth. "Lick it," he orders. "Make it nice and wet for me."

I shudder with desire, and do as he says, wetting my palm with my own saliva. Then Sebastian wraps it around his thick girth, showing me how to grip and move to please him. "Tighter, yes. Like that. Faster. Fuck, yes."

Oh God. I breathlessly follow his commands, jerking him off, pressing the blunt head of his cock against my clit with every stroke as I rock and grind against him.

"Does that feel good?" Sebastian groans.

"Yes," I gasp, thrusting my hips, chasing the sweet friction. "God, yes!"

"That's my girl. You like it raw, don't you? Like to see what you do to me."

He's right. Our eyes are locked, both of us breathing heavier now, it's dirty and fast; pure instinct pushing me on. I'm the one setting the pace this time. I'm the one making him pant and moan, even as my own pleasure rises, spiraling out of control. I feel like I'm on the edge of madness, my desire for him on full display.

Then he yanks my panties to the side and sinks his fingers inside of me. I tip back my head and cry out in pleasure. Fuck, it feels incredible, he's pulsing thickly from within me as I grind my clit, messy against his cock. The crest is close, so close—

Sebastian leans in and sucks my nipple into his mouth,

pulling hard on the stiff nub, a sharp burst of pressure so sweet, I start to come undone—

He bites down, and I shatter with a scream, clenching around his fingers as he curses my name, pumps once, twice, into my hand and then comes in a liquid rush of heat, flooding onto my belly.

I sink against him, reeling. Slowly, Sebastian withdraws his fingers, and then licks them clean. "You're still so tight," he murmurs appreciatively. "You'll have to stretch to take it. But when I'm done with you, you'll be ready for every last inch."

I shiver, though I'm not sure if it's because of fear...

Or pure, pulse-racing desire.

Chapter 16

Avery

The next few days pass in a whirl of research—and passion. Sebastian is busy with work, so I'm able to steal away to the library every day under the guise of shopping or spa time. Luckily, he doesn't seem to expect anything more from me, or wonder if I'm bored with all the endless beauty treatments.

Apparently, this is how the women in his world pass their time.

Me? I prefer vengeance.

I'm focused now, learning as much as I can about Sebastian. He's a cutthroat businessman. Companies have been destroyed and rivals ruined. I make notes of all of it, searching for potential enemies, or a weakness of some kind. The list of people he's fucked over is a long one, but nothing screams 'opportunity' to me just yet. Most of them are wise enough to slink off, and never show their faces again.

I need more than that. I need a silver bullet that can pierce Sebastian's armor and embed it straight in his heart.

So, my days are full of planning. But my nights?

My nights still belong to him.

Sebastian's lessons continue—and I can't get enough. He takes me to the edge, drives me crazy, and teaches my body things that I never dreamed about, leaving me gasping and satisfied, but he hasn't even attempted to take things further. It's like there's an invisible line that he won't cross.

I'm not sure if I want him to or not. Or at least, I'm not sure how I'll deal with it emotionally when we come to that moment. Right now, I'm trying to build my defenses, harden my mind against him even as my body writhes and gasps in pleasure. But how long can I keep up this double life?

Sooner or later, something's going to crack.

"We're almost there."

Sebastian's voice interrupts my thoughts. For once, he's behind the wheel, and I'm in the passenger seat of his classic silver Aston Martin. We're driving out to the countryside today, to visit his mom and uncle at their home, which I'm hoping is an opportunity to uncover more about his past.

The whole, weird Wolfe family.

So far, the drive has passed in companionable silence. It's a bright, clear day, and I've been drinking in the views of the country, as the city made way for rolling fields and pretty woodland, the further we drive from London.

Now, I turn to Sebastian, ready to start my subtle inquisition. He's dressed down today, in dark-wash jeans and a cashmere sweater, but he's still the most commanding presence I've known.

"So... What's the deal with your mom and uncle, exactly?" I venture, "They're together now?"

Sebastian doesn't look over. "Yes."

His tone is clipped. He's been acting casual about this visit, but the closer we get to our destination, the more tension I can sense coming from him.

"That must have been weird for you, after your dad passed and everything."

He gives a shrug. "They grew closer, after Dad died. Richard was very supportive. They married about ten years ago."

Okaaay.

I can't believe anyone would be chill with their uncle marrying their mom, but apparently, Sebastian is pretending it's all fine with him.

We'll see about that.

My research has told me that after Patrick Wolfe died in a car accident, his brother, Richard stepped in, and ran Wolfe Capital—until Sebastian came of age to take the reins. According to what I've read in the papers, they're all one big happy family, but I clocked some serious tension at dinner, and I can't wait to see the vibes up close.

Maybe I should try to stir the pot and see what happens.

After another half-hour of driving, Sebastian turns off the motorway, and down a series of winding country lanes. We pass some pretty villages, but he doesn't slow, roaring along at break-neck speed until we turn through a pair of modern looking gates, and down a long driveway.

"Wow," I blink, as the house comes into view. I was expecting something grand and historic, and this is impressive, sure, but glaringly modern: a boxy new concrete mansion in the midst of the countryside, all sharp angles and looming windows. "It's... Big."

"The biggest private residence in the county." Sebastian says, but his tone is unreadable. Still, he doesn't seem overjoyed about coming to visit his family.

He pulls up in front of the imposing main doors, just as Sebastian's mother, Trudy, comes out to greet us, dressed in that English country look: riding boots, tweed, and a crisp button-down. "Here you are!" she declares, giving Sebastian a brief kiss on the cheek, before turning to me with a big smile. "And Avery, it's so nice to see you again."

"Thanks for inviting us, Mrs. Wolfe."

"Call me Trudy, please."

I smile. "Okay, Trudy."

"And you," she says, turning to Sebastian. "Do I need to give you a tour of the place? You never visit, so I don't know if you remember the layout."

Sebastian sighs. "You know I'm busy."

"Well, at least you've finally brought a girl home. I was starting to think you were too embarrassed to introduce me to anyone."

She leads us inside, which is just as impressive: all double-height ceilings and glass walls, with poured concrete floors and chic furniture. "How was the drive, Richard says the traffic's terrible these days out of the city—"

Sebastian's phone sounds with a sharp buzz. He pulls it out, and then answers. "Yes?" he barks. "No, that's not what I said. Listen carefully..."

He turns and disappears into the house to talk, sounding irritated.

"Anyone would think I never taught him manners," Trudy tuts. "Business has always come first with that boy. But now, I can't leave you all alone, and I need to run into town for some bits and pieces for dinner."

"But if you need to leave, don't worry about me," I reassure her. "I can entertain myself."

"Are you sure?"

"Of course. I'll take a walk and enjoy the country air."

"You're a darling," she says. "The estate goes all the way to the lake on that side, and the road on the other, wander away. I won't be long!"

Trudy heads out, leaving me alone. I poke my head into a few rooms, seeing a curious mix of overstuffed, old looking furniture with all the new modern pieces. But Sebastian is still somewhere in the house, and I'm not about to start rifling through any drawers, so, I follow through on my line to Trudy, and head out the back door to take that walk, glad I wore flat boots and brought a jacket.

There's a path, of sorts, leading away from the house and up a hill, so I stroll, enjoying the greenery, and peace and quiet. Here, it's trees all the way to the horizon, and I can barely pick out rooftops across the stretch of fields.

So what's Sebastian's deal here? I'm trying to figure out of the tense vibes I'm picking up on. Trudy was being passive-aggressive with Sebastian about not visiting, so is his issue with her, or Richard.

Or the both of them. Despite his shrugs in the car, that has to be weird for him.

And is there a connection to Sebastian's dad's death? Clearly, it's a big deal, but is it just regular family trauma stemming from a loss... Or is it something I can use against him?

At the very least, I might be able to get Sebastian's guard down over it. I'll take any advantage I can get.

"Well, hello there!"

The sound of a man's voice startles me. I've circled back around the house and find Richard on the path to what looks like a workshop or office. He's wearing a Barbour jacket and boots, every inch the country gentleman.

"Oh, hi," I blurt. "I didn't see you there."

"Sorry to scare you." He gives me a big, toothy grin. "Trudy said that you lovebirds were coming this afternoon. I haven't seen Sebastian yet, though."

"He's around here somewhere, taking an important business phone call."

"Ah. That must have something to do with the Dunleavey deal."

I think about the nice older couple we met for lunch and almost lose my smile. Sebastian was so cold when he talked about taking over the man's company.

"I wouldn't know," I say with a smile. "All of that finance stuff goes way over my head."

Richard chuckles. "Wise girl, it's nothing but a headache. Were you heading back in?"

I nod, and he falls into step beside me. "You know, it's good to see Seb with someone like you," Richard remarks warmly. "Maybe you can get him to lighten up and stop taking life so seriously."

"He is very focused on work," I agree, neutral.

"To a fault," Richard says. "I sometimes think it brings out the worst in him. All this cutthroat business dealing, it's not good for the soul. And Sebastian's... well. He has a tendency of pursuing his victories, not matter the cost. To him, or the people around him."

I don't reply. Everything Richard is saying is true, but I wonder why he's telling me. Is it just more 'friendly advice' like Becca was giving me back in the city, or is Richard trying to put a wedge between me and Sebastian?

It's like nobody in his life has a good word to say about him.

But am I really surprised about that?

Trudy returns with groceries, and Sebastian finishes his calls. Soon, we're all seated for dinner in the grand dining room, on either side of a massive concrete table that could seat two dozen people.

"So, Avery, I want to hear all about you." Trudy beams,

over the roast beef. "Tell me everything, where did you grow up? What about your family? What brings you to England?"

I take a long sip of wine to get my story straight. "Well, I grew up in upstate New York..." I begin.

It's harder than I thought it would be to remember everything about my false identity—plus be tactful about how I met Sebastian, too, and there are a few times when I'm slow to answer as my mind frantically sorts the truth from the fabricated story, but I don't think anyone notices.

"And how are you liking London?" Richard asks.

"It's great. I go out exploring every day."

"And what is it you do, exactly?"

Plot to destroy your son—when I'm not orgasming around his skilled fingers and tongue.

I flush. "Mostly just shopping and going to the spa or salon," I say with a little giggle. "I've done a little sightseeing too."

"Has Sebastian taken you to the London Eye? I hear that tourists love it."

I try to imagine Sebastian out with a 'I heart London' T-shirt, and stifle a grin. "Actually, he's been busy with work, so..."

"Ah," Richard cuts in, smiling in a smug way. "That's not surprising. It's tough to run a business like Wolfe Capital, especially the way things are at the minute."

"What do you mean?" Sebastian's voice is crisp.

"Just that these are uncertain economic times." Richard sips his wine. "A place like Wolfe needs a steady hand at the tiller, to keep the troops in line."

"You're rather mixing your metaphors, aren't you?" Sebastian shoots back.

Richard chuckles. "You know what I mean. It's a bad time to be taking big risks."

"And if my father had followed your advice to play it safe,

he never would have started the company. So, I rather think risk-taking is in the Wolfe DNA. *Our* DNA, anyway."

There's a moment of heavy silence before Trudy changes the subject. "I'm thinking of redecorating the kitchen!" she announces brightly. "What do you think about green tile? I saw some gorgeous ones, handmade in Provence, and they have the most exquisite ranges, too..." She chatters on, acting so natural, as if she has to redirect the conversation like this all the time.

I just focus on my food, but I can feel the coiled irritation radiating from Sebastian at my side. Even as Trudy engages everyone in polite conversation, there's a heaviness in the air that makes me eager to get away from the table.

Talk about family dysfunction.

Finally, the meal comes to an end. "Nightcap, anyone?" Trudy asks.

"No. Thank you." Sebastian replies, getting to his feet. "It's been a long day. We're turning in."

I guess we are.

"Thank you for dinner," I say to his mom, before following Sebastian to the stairs. He pauses.

"You go ahead. I have more calls. I'll be up shortly."

The room we're staying in is large and airy, with a modern ensuite. I get changed into a silky nightgown and matching robe and wait for him.

But he doesn't come.

The hours tick past. I watch TV shows on my phone to kill the time, but eventually, as midnight rolls around, I decide to go find him.

The house is dark. Trudy and Richard have clearly turned in for the night, so I tiptoe through the dim hallways, not wanting to disturb anyone. I head downstairs, and wander, until I see a light coming from under a doorway at the far end of the hall.

Peeking inside, I find a library. Sebastian is sitting in an armchair by the fireplace, gazing into the flickering flames.

I pause. I've never seen him like this before—alone, with his own thoughts. The usual cool and reserved way he holds himself is gone. He looks almost *vulnerable*.

I feel a strange tightness in my chest, but quickly push it aside. I don't have any pity for the man. *This is my opportunity*. Because if he's feeling emotional for some reason right now, it's my chance to get beneath his walls.

I push open the door and walk inside.

Chapter 17

Sebastian

I shouldn't have come here.

I'm not sure why I did. My mother is always inviting me, and I always find an excuse.. I'm busy enough, running the Wolfe Capital empire, and I see her from time to time in London, so it's not as if she can say I'm avoiding her.

But here, in the house my father built... It's hard for me to keep the memories at bay.

Memories, and *guilt*.

Maybe I thought bringing Avery here would make it easier, that I would be calmed by her sunny presence and sinful curves. But even though I know she's waiting for me upstairs, laying in my bed, ready for another sensual lesson, I linger here by the fire.

I can't see her like this. Off-balance, distracted. *Weak.*

I take another swallow of my whisky, staring into the fire. This used to be a home, a place of safety and comfort. Now, it feels like it's haunted, with dark secrets lurking down every corridor.

Secrets that can never, ever be brought into the light.

There's a creak in the doorway, and I look up to see Avery venturing into the room. "Are you OK?" she asks, watching me with those wide eyes. She's wrapped in a thin robe, her hair falling loose around her shoulders, and a sleepy expression on her face. She looks beautiful, like a precious thing that my dirty hands don't deserve to even touch.

It makes me want to possess her even more. Prove that nothing can stop me from taking what I want, even if I'm not fit to taste her sweetness.

"Come here," I beckon, and she does what I say, obediently crossing the room to me. I pull her onto my lap, and she tenses a moment, before gingerly curling against me, resting her head against my shoulder.

I take a deep breath, breathing in the light, lemon scent of her shampoo. Like sunshine. Avery slowly relaxes in my arms, and I feel a curious sense of peace. Odd. I've made the girl moan, and gasp, and come screaming my name, my face between her legs and my fingers buried in her tight cunt.... But this feels more intimate than any of it.

When was the last time I simply held someone?

We sit there in silence for a moment, just watching the fire. Avery doesn't try to make me talk, and for that, I'm glad.

Somehow, holding her is enough to keep the memories at bay.

"My father had this house built for us," I find myself telling her.

Avery twists in my lap, so she's looking up at me.

"I told you, he was from a humble background," I continue quietly. "He'd always dreamed of having a big, impressive house one day. So when the company took off, he started looking. He planned to buy a big stately manor from some aristocrats, but they took their house off the market rather than sell it to him."

"Why?" Avery asks, frowning.

"Because they were old money, and we weren't." I give a twisted smile at the memory. "That's when Dad realized, he could never buy his way into the upper classes here, no matter how many millions he made."

"So what happened?"

"He said, fuck them all."

Avery giggles in shock, and I smile, too, remembering my dad's brash attitude. "He wouldn't scrape, and bootlick to win over people who would never respect him. He decided to go his own way, not play by their snooty rules. He had this place designed for us and never looked back. Everything newer, and bigger, and better than the competition, that was his thinking."

"It clearly worked out."

I nod. "It's my philosophy too. Be progressive, move forward. It doesn't matter what people say or think about you. Cash is king. When you're rich enough, powerful enough... Well, nobody can say 'No' to you then."

I bought that historical estate in the end. Took over out the company that held the mortgage, then drove the owner damn near to bankruptcy, until he had no choice but to sell. For half the price my dad would have paid.

He learned, alright. I don't forgive an insult.

Avery gets up and strolls over to the bookshelves. "Are these your books?" she asks.

"Some, from when I was growing up. My dad's mostly. This was his favorite room in the house. For all his talk about new being better, he loved old books."

She browses the shelves for a while, then pulls out a book for a closer look. Avery lets out a laugh. "Interesting vintage collection you have here," she teases. "Nancy Drew, Sweet Valley High, Baby-Sitters Club..."

I pause. "Those were my sister's."

Avery blinks. "Sister?" she repeats in surprise. "I didn't know you have any siblings."

I choose my words carefully, already regretting that I've revealed so much. "Scarlett was born when I was seven years old, and she loved to read."

My use of the past tense isn't lost on Avery. Her expression floods with sympathy. "I'm sorry for bringing her up," she says quietly. "I know how hard it can be to lose to someone you love."

That's right, her father.

Avery traces the book spines, looking distant. "You think you've moved on, that you've come to terms with missing them, and then... Something small happens, you know, a song comes on the radio that they loved, or you hear something that you want to tell them about, and you remember they're gone... all over again."

She looks at me, and something flashes in her eyes. Almost like pure rage. But it's gone in an instant, so fast, I wonder if I misread it. Avery gives a self-conscious laugh, "Sorry, listen to me, rambling on. I don't mean to be such a buzzkill."

"You can be anything you want," I say without thinking. "You don't have to pretend with me."

Again, there's a flash of something on her face, but it's quickly replaced with a flirty smile. "You mean, you don't want me faking it with you?"

Heat snakes through me. She's in front of the fire now, the light glowing through her robe, illuminating every one of her delicious curves. "Oh, you couldn't fake it if you tried," I reply, getting to my feet. I move to her, "I know this body, remember?" I slide my hands over her ass, yanking her against me.

Avery gasps, color rising to her cheeks. Fuck, I love how responsive she is. I can already read her like a book. "You think you could fake *this*?" I murmur, tracing my fingertips over her collarbone, so she shivers, her skin pebbling in tiny goosebumps. "Or this?" I palm her breasts, squeezing until her nipples protrude in stiff peaks.

"Or how wet you get when I do this?"

I bury my hand in her hair, and then grip it in a rough handful, forcing her head to one side and grazing the length of her neck with my teeth.

Avery gives a helpless moan, arching her body against me even as I keep up the tight grip in her hair.

She loves it when I take control. And fuck, it ignites something inside me too. Something primal and raw, the urge to dominate her completely, and claim her body without mercy. Leave her messy and whimpering, begging my name.

Because I'm the only one who can make her feel this way.

The only one she'll ever need.

I pick her up easily, dragging her down to lay on the antique rug in front of the fire. Avery stares up at me, flushed and breathing fast beneath me. "What are you doing?" she whispers, her eyes wide with excitement.

"Wrong question," I growl, moving down her body. "Try again."

She flushes even deeper, biting her lip. "What do you want me to do?" she finally asks, and fuck, my cock gets hard just from the breathless obedience in her voice.

She's learning fast just what I want from her—and how much she likes it.

"Hike up your nightgown and spread your legs for me," I order, already hungry to taste her again.

Avery sends a fearful glance over to where she left the door to the library wide open. "But... Aren't you going to close the door?"

"No." I shove her thighs roughly apart, and sound a low

groan when I find her, bare and glistening for me. "No panties? Naughty girl."

Avery stifles a moan as my hands slide higher. But she's still laying there, tense, watching the doorway. "Sebastian, we can't... What if someone hears? Your mom, or Richard..."

Nobody tells me what the fuck I can't do.

I nip her inner thigh with my teeth. Hard. Avery gasps. "Then you'll just have to keep quiet now, won't you? Think you can do that for me?" I command. "Keep that pretty voice of yours silent with my tongue in your cunt?"

I don't wait for her answer, I just bury my face between her legs.

Avery arches off the rug with a gasp, but I push her back down, pinning her in place with a hand on her stomach while my tongue goes to town on her sweet cunt.

Fuck, this girl is delicious, and so wet, she's a dream. I lap at her pussy, playing with her clit until Avery is stifling whimpers, writhing above me. Then I spear my tongue inside her, and she can't help but cry out.

I smile in victory at the ragged sound, echoing in the dark house. I don't care if anyone finds us, but I know it makes Avery hotter, having the threat of discovery hanging over her.

Yes, this girl has some interesting kinks buried beneath her innocent surface. I'm learning more about her every day. Discovery, public places... When I found her on that balcony at the party, and finger-fucked her where anyone could see...

She'd never been wetter.

And when I gripped her throat and started squeezing...?

She went off like a firework, blazing and raw.

It's intoxicating, taking her to the edge like that, bulldozing every last boundary until she's screaming for more. She still thinks she needs to fight me—and herself. To pretend like she doesn't want what I do to her body, that she doesn't long for the pleasure I provide. I see it in her eyes, every time. The resistance, the way she wrestles with her body's response to me, trying to keep control.

It's amusing, how little she understands her own desire.

Because what Avery doesn't realize, is that she craves her own surrender. To let go, and submit completely to me—that's what takes her over the edge, every damn time. She can fight all she wants, but that moment where the fight leaves her body, and she finally gives in and offers up possession of her pleasure to me?

That's what she needs to get her off.

Obedience.

And I'll take it from her, every time. She's writhing against my mouth now, tensing in a way that tells me she's close to climax. "Oh God," she moans, in that sexy pant that makes me even harder. "Please, Sebastian, right there!"

I give her clit another few licks, hearing the pitch of her voice rise higher, her body twisting tighter—

And then I pull away.

Avery sobs in frustration, lifting her head. "But, why?" she blurts, pink-cheeked and so damn flustered, I almost want to finish the job, just to ease her distress.

But that's not what she needs from me.

She needs a firm hand, not a fucking boyfriend.

"Wrong question," I say coolly, rocking back on my heels. "Try again."

Avery's eyes widen in realization. She scrambles to sit up, her body still trembling from my expert strokes. "What do you want me to do?"

Again, her halting obedience goes straight to my cock. And this time, we're going to do something about that.

I unbuckle my belt. "Suck me off," I order her roughly.

"And maybe if you're good enough, I'll give you a reward, and let you come."

Avery glances to the open door, blushing deeper, but she crawls over to me, and eagerly fumbles with my pants. She's too turned on now to even think of putting up a fight, and fuck, the sight of her on all fours, her pink lips opening wide and swallowing my cock down makes me swell even harder.

"Fuck, yes." I groan, as the wet heat of her mouth slides over me, "All the way, you can take it. That's my good girl, every fucking inch."

My lust is roaring through me now, a wild beast unleashed by her tight suction and nimble tongue. I bury a hand in her hair and yank her to take me deeper. Avery lets out a sob of protest, struggling to take me all the way, but I don't ease up, I don't let her even adjust to the punishing girth of me, I just thrust into her deeper, faster, fucking her mouth relentlessly as I grip her hair, controlling her movements completely until she's limp and moaning in pleasure, a willing vessel for my cock.

Mine.

I yank up her nightgown and land a stinging slap on her perfect ass. Avery moans around my cock, and then wriggles her ass, wanting more even as she struggles to swallow me down.

Fuck. It takes me over, the fierce possession, raging in my bloodstream as I spank her again, harder, making her sob and moan with my cock in her mouth as my climax builds to a fucking crescendo. I'm consumed by this girl, ravaged, weak for the pleasure only she can provide. *She's mine. She has to be. All mine—*

I come with a roar, exploding down her tight throat in a hot burst of pleasure, and dammit, Avery swallows every drop, milking me dry as the force of my release spears through me, so damn good, my brain whites out, and for one blissful moment, I'm free.

Free from the past, and all my secrets. Free from the guilt and shame I carry every minute of every day.

Except this one. With her. Only Avery can make it all go away.

How the hell does she do this to me?

Chapter 18

Avery

Back in London, Sebastian disappears, practically living at the office again. I'm relieved. I need space to focus on my research—and to process everything that happened in the country.

The night in the library together... It still makes my thighs clench with lust whenever I think about it, but the whole thing unsettled me, too. Sebastian was a man untamed: animalistic and raw. Usually, he's so controlled. Even in the grip of pleasure, he keeps his distance, icy and detached. But this...?

He was still in control, demanding everything I had to give, but he was unravelling, too. And God, it turned me on to see him that way, feeling the rough grip of his hands grip my hair, and the sting of his palm against my ass. But now that I've had some time to process, I realize what's unnerving me about that night.

I saw a glimpse of the darkness, lurking inside him. A man who'll go to any lengths to get what he wants. It chills and tempts me, all at the same time.

Maybe Sebastian knows he revealed too much, because he's

barely touched me since. No more sensual lessons, no more filthy commands. Every night, I wonder if I'll hear his knock on the bedroom door.

And every night, I find myself wishing that I would.

Which is crazy—and dangerous. Because the next time he comes for me, he won't settle for just getting me off with his hands, and mouth, and dirty words. He'll want more of me.

All of me.

And I don't know yet if that's a price I'm willing to pay.

"Good morning," I greet Leon, heading downstairs for breakfast, a few days after we arrive back in London.

"Mornin'," he replies, still stern-faced as ever. "Coffee?"

"Yes please," I smile. "And some of those amazing crepes, if they're on the menu?"

He nods. "Mr. Wolfe just finished his breakfast. I believe he's on a call."

Big surprise.

I make my way through to the dining room. I can see Sebastian from here, pacing in the back gardens, angrily gesturing to whoever's unfortunate enough to be on the other end of that call. He's totally absorbed and doesn't even look up to see me.

I pause, thinking fast. If he's out there, distracted...

His office. This could be my chance.

I quickly hurry out, and down the hallway. Sure enough, his office door is ajar, as if he just strolled out. It's set to the side of the house, so doesn't have a view to the gardens. There's no chance of him seeing me, so I slip inside, and look around.

There are papers stacked on his desk, different files open, and a pile of opened mail.

Jackpot.

I move to the desk. His laptop has already gone into sleep

mode, so I don't risk touching it, but as for the rest of the papers, I skim them quickly, looking for anything interesting. Business proposals... investor reports... There's a credit card statement, with eye-popping amounts charged to different hotels and designer stores in Europe. Payroll to the household staff. A file of invoices from some kind of trust account, with bank transfer records—

Wait a minute.

I pull the file closer. There are household bills for an address in Sussex, and bank statements showing a single transaction every month: Thousands of pounds going to someone called S. Whitley. The statements go back years, and buried towards the back of the file, there are invoices from a business called Larkspur Services Incorporated, dated from over a decade ago.

I'm not sure what any of this is, but I don't have much time to figure it out right now. I grab a loose sheet of paper from the printer, and quickly jot down any names and addresses that I see. Then I position everything where I left it, and hurry back to the door. I peer out. All clear.

I'm just walking back to the dining room as casually as I can, when Becca appears in the hallway. She's got a piece of toast in one hand, and a contract in the other. She looks up, surprised. "What are you doing here?"

"I live here," I reply, my heart pounding. I slip the paper into my pocket as Becca looks past me, to Sebastian's office.

The only other place I could have been.

"Have you seen Sebastian?" I blurt quickly. "I was just looking for him."

"He's out back, on a call," she replies, still looking at me suspiciously.

"Great," I beam. "Thanks so much."

I make to move past her, but Becca blocks my path, and

narrows her eyes. "I don't know what you're playing at, but I do know that you're not as innocent as you seem."

My stomach lurches in fear, but I keep my composure. Old Avery would smack her for saying something like that or threaten to end her. New Avery wouldn't dream of it. "Wow, what an odd thing to say," I manage to reply, wide-eyed. "And pretty rude, too, to be honest." I smile at her. "Would you mind getting out of the way? Sebastian loves having breakfast with me. He'll be wondering where I am."

She stands aside, and I make it back to the dining room, my pulse racing, just as Leon brings in my breakfast. Sebastian enters via the garden, striding through the French doors.

"Everything okay?" I ask brightly, hoping that my face isn't flushed with the spike of my adrenaline.

He gives a curt nod. "What are your plans for the day?"

"Oh, you know. Shopping, maybe a massage." I give a careless shrug, as if the only thing on my mind is where to find some cute shoes.

"Feel free to stop at the lingerie shop again," Sebastian gives me a wicked look. "Or perhaps there are other *toys* you could enjoy buying..."

I inhale in a rush at the thought. Clearly, Sebastian's done staying out of my bedroom.

"Perhaps," I offer, flirty. "Any suggestions?"

His gaze darkens. "Why don't you surprise me?"

"Oh, I will," I reply, thinking of the slip of paper in my back pocket. When I finally bring him down, and reveal what I've been doing all along, Sebastian will get one hell of a surprise.

Back at the library, I greet Linda, the desk clerk, by name. we're practically old friends now. "What can I get for you today?" she asks, smiling.

"Some more back issues of *Fortune* and *Business Weekly,* I'm afraid," I tell her, rattling off the next issues I've flagged on my list. "And more computer time, if anything's available."

"We're pretty full today, but I'll see what I can do."

She goes check, as someone joins me at the desk. "Sounds like you're working on a big project," he says.

I turn. A guy in his twenties with sandy hair and wire-rimmed glasses is smiling at me, friendly.

"Uh... Yeah. It's a research paper," I explain, as Linda returns with my stack of magazines and the login information for the computer.

The guy chuckles, as I balance everything in my arms. "Well, you certainly take the research part seriously. I'm James, by the way," he says, holding out his hand, then dropping it when he realizes that I can't shake it.

I give an awkward flutter of a wave, instead. "Hi, I'm Avery."

"Nice to meet you, Avery. Need any help?" he offers.

"Thanks, I've got it," I tell him. "Well, I better get started, before someone grabs my computer time."

"Oh, yes, you can't dawdle. It's cutthroat out there," he cracks. "I've seen people come to blows in the periodical section."

"Really?" I blink.

"Polite blows," he corrects himself. "More like nudges. With plenty of apologies."

I laugh again. There's something about his earnest smile that makes me think of Miles. And then I feel it, that same familiar pang of grief that always comes when I think of him.

I shift the magazines in my arms. "Nice to meet you, James." I nod again, and head for my study carrell.

Focus, Avery. You can't waste any time.

Getting to work, I start by browsing through the newspapers. I've flagged any article that mentions Sebastian or the company, but I don't find much scandal there, and I'm starting to wonder if I've exhausted this resource.

Turning to the computer, I decide to investigate the information I found today. I pull out my slip of scribbled information and start with one of the names on the paperwork I found.

Larkspur Services Incorporated.

I put it in the search bar and check the results.

It's a psychiatric facility.

What?

I had no idea what to expect, but this is a shock. Did Sebastian have some kind of breakdown? Or someone close to him? The invoices were from a decade ago, so it could have been anyone.

Feeling like I might finally be on the right track, I check the address in Sussex next. Sebastian's been paying household bills there for years through an anonymous trust, and it looks like it's just a residential home. I do a little digging, but I find out that it last sold ten years ago. The information I find doesn't list a buyer at that time, but I have to wonder if it was Sebastian. Why else would he be paying the bills there?

And why would he hide it, not in his own name?

I pull up image searches and find some photos of the house. It's a pretty little cottage with stables in the middle of nowhere. Not exactly Sebastian's lavish style.

I sit back and think hard. I knew from my experience with the Barretti crime family that large amounts of money like this are usually used to hide something juicy. Skeletons people want to stay, deep in the closet.

Blackmail? A payoff? A secret child?

That thought is accompanied by an unwelcome twinge of jealousy. I force myself to ignore it. What I need to focus on is whatever—or whoever—is down in Sussex.

If Sebastian is hiding something there, it could be the key to everything.

My alarm on my phone buzzes, reminding me it's time to get back to Bond Street, especially if I'm going to pick up some random purchases to keep my cover story straight. Reluctantly, I pack up my stuff and turn in the newspapers before heading for the exit.

I've just stepped outside, when I hear a voice behind me. "Wait up!"

I turn. It's James, the guy from before. He catches up to me. "I think you dropped this," he says, holding out a fancy looking fountain pen.

I shake my head. "Thanks, but that's not mine."

"Oh, OK. I thought it might be your lucky pen, or maybe I'm the only geek who has one of those," he adds, looking bashful.

I laugh.

"I wish I was joking," James continues. "It's this red ballpoint, and I swear, I almost failed my history finals because I left it at home."

"Almost," I say. "That means you did just fine without it."

"I mean, I'm a penniless post-doc student, so I don't know how 'fine' things turned out for me." James grins. "But I do have money for coffee, if you'd like one?" he nods to the coffee cart, set up on the sidewalk.

I hesitate, but I have some time before I should meet the driver. "Sure." I decide.

We walk over and order our drinks, although I insist on paying for mine. "So, I take it you're not from around here?" he asks.

"I know, the accent is a dead giveaway, right?" I make a face.

"It's cute," he says.

I pause. "Thanks," I reply, careful. I give him a sideways glance. Is he flirting with me?

James looks at me and smiles. "Wait, hold still, you have something in your hair." Before I can react, he reaches out, and plucks a piece of lint from it. "Rolling in a laundry pile, huh?"

"Sure, I do it all the time."

OK, he's definitely flirting, which means I need to shut this down.

James clears his throat, looking nervous. "Listen, I don't know if you have any plans tonight, but..."

Oh, no. I hopes he's not about to ask me out.

"... There's this party I'm going to. Just a casual thing," he adds quickly, "Some other students I know, it should be fun. If you'd like to come?"

I give him a polite smile. "Sorry. I have plans. With my boyfriend," I add gently.

He coughs. "Wow, screwed that one up, huh?"

"No, I mean, I'm flattered. But, busy."

"Well, until next time." James says, raising his coffee in a toast. "I better get back to it. And see who's missing their lucky pen," he adds.

I smile. Maybe in another world, I could have stuck around, and gone with him to that party. But I'm not some research student, flirting over coffee.

I'm on a mission, and with today's breakthrough, I'm closer to my prize than ever before.

When I arrive at the house that evening, I'm surprised to find Sebastian back from the office early. And even more shocking, he's set up a romantic dinner for the two of us: white linens, candlelight, champagne on ice...

"What's the occasion?" I ask, greeting him. I kiss his cheek automatically, seeing that his hair is damp from the shower. He's barefoot, in jeans and a button-down shirt that's open at his neck, and is that...?

Yes, a smile on his face.

I blink. "Who are you, and what have you done with the surly, demanding Sebastian I've seen all week?" I can't help asking, a teasing note in my voice.

Sebastian chuckles. "I have been rather an ass, haven't I? I get like that, when it comes to closing a deal. Are you hungry?"

I nod. "Starved. I forgot to eat lunch."

"Shopping as a competitive sport, hmm?"

Shit. I give a little laugh to cover, as Sebastian hands me a plate. "These should tide you over, until the main event is ready."

I look down to find... pizza bagels?

I laugh, and Sebastian looks smug. "You asked Leon to order them. A foreign delicacy?"

"I have a sophisticated palate," I inform him, airy. Then I take a big bite. "Try one," I offer him the plate.

He chuckles, taking one. "Not bad," he says, chewing. "But I prefer caviar as an appetizer."

"Of course you do."

"How about some music before dinner?" Sebastian says casually.

"Sure." I follow him to the living room, munching happily on my pizza bagels—

I freeze in the doorway. "What is that?" I breathe in disbelief.

"This?" Sebastian looks even more smug. "Just your new piano."

My... What?

I drift forward, taking in what has to be the most beautiful instrument I've ever seen. "But... This is a Fazioli," I whisper, recognizing the emblem of the famed maker. I reach out and stroke the polished surface with my fingertips.

Sebastian smiles. "Sit. Get a feel for it."

I sink onto the stool in disbelief, tentatively putting my fingers to the keys. I've never even touched anything like this. Fazioli pianos cost over two hundred thousand dollars, and from the feel of it, they're worth every penny.

"Play something," Sebastian says, still watching me from across the room.

I take a deep breath. I can't overthink it, otherwise I'll never feel like anything I play would be worthy of this great instrument, so I close my eyes and play the first thing that pops into my mind, *All of Me* by John Legend. For a few moments, the world melts away, and it's just me and the music, and my voice, in the quiet of the room.

Then I finish, and come back to reality again, flushed.

I snatch my hands away. "Sorry," I blurt.

Sebastian raises his eyebrows. "What for?"

"Nothing, I just... I'm not good enough to play something like this."

"Says who?"

I give a short laugh. "Uh, anyone with a set of ears?" I stroke the keyboard reverently. "Something like this is meant for real musicians."

"It's meant for anyone I say," he replies arrogantly. "And I say it's yours."

I study him. He's watching me, sipping his wine, and actually seems... happy. "I've never seen you like this," I remark, smiling.

"That's because you've never seen me when I close a deal." Sebastian takes a long sip. "Play something else," he instructs me, but I pause, wary.

"What deal?" I ask.

"The Dunleavey matter," Sebastian strolls closer, setting his glass on the top of the piano. And I'm so focused on his words, I can't even tell him to move it in case he leaves a mark.

"You finally arranged the partnership with Alistair?" I ask.

Sebastian smirks. "No. The old fool wouldn't take a good deal when he saw one. So, I staged a hostile takeover. As of tonight, Wolfe Capital owns a controlling stake in Dunleavey shipping." He smiles, pleased. "With the real estate assets and machinery, I'll be able to strip the company for parts and make a nice profit."

"Strip it?" I echo, shocked. "But what about the business? All the employees? Alistair said at lunch, it's a family company."

"Was," Sebastian corrects me. "Now, it's mine, and I'll run it as I see fit. Which means losing most of the workforce—and management, too. Dead weight," he says with a shrug. "They've held on long enough."

I stare at him, sickened by the casual cruelty in his tone. "Those are people's lives," I say quietly. "How can you talk about them like that?"

Sebastian shrugs. "Easily."

"You have no right," I tell him angrily.

"I have every right," he replies. "It says it right there in the contracts, next to the eighty million I just invested. My money, my rules."

I shake my head, disgusted. "I forgot, we're all just property to you."

I get up, and stalk for the door. I can't look at him for another minute, but Sebastian catches my wrist and yanks me back to him.

"Let me go," I demand angrily.

"Not tonight, Little Sparrow." Sebastian pins me against the piano, claiming my mouth in a cruel kiss. I struggle against him, trying to push him away, but his kiss is merciless, tongue pushing deep between my lips, like he's claiming ownership of me.

Like everything else.

I bite down on his lip. Hard.

Sebastian finally pulls away, gingerly touching where I bit him. He gives a bitter laugh. "You don't want to test me right now," he says, warning.

"Or what?" I demand, my heart pounding. "I thought you didn't force women?"

Sebastian arches an eyebrow. "I don't need to force you, remember? You've already proven just how willing you can be with the right... *instructions*. So what will it be tonight, Sparrow?" he muses, his expression sneering as he looks over me from head to toe. "Will I tell you to get on your knees and suck me off like a good girl? Or maybe you'll put on a little show for me, strip naked for my pleasure while I decide where I'm going to reward you with my cum. You'd like that, wouldn't you?" he growls, stalking closer to me. "Earning your pleasure from me. Begging so sweetly for release."

I feel an involuntary flush of lust, even as my blood boils with anger. "No," I blurt, shaking my head. "We're not doing any of that."

"Why not?" he demands. "You want it. I can see, remember? Your body doesn't lie to me."

He reaches out to squeeze my breast. I slap his hand away.

"You think I could be with you, want you, after what you just did? You're a monster!" I cry.

"Yes." Sebastian growls, backing me up again. He pins me in place, and touches me again, his hand palming and squeezing, toying with my aching nipples that are already stiff with desire.

I bite back a moan, hating myself.

"Nothing's changed." Sebastian tells me harshly, his hands taking ownership of my body. My pleasure. "Tonight is no different from any other night you've begged for me. I'm still the same man. The same monster. You've known it all along."

I shake my head, but I can't deny it.

And Sebastian knows.

His hand moves roughly between my legs, petting me there, as he grips my jaw in one hand, watching my helpless reaction to him. "See?" he growls, tilting my chin up painfully. "You still want me, despite everything. Or maybe... Because of it."

A rush of shame spirals through me, or maybe it's desire. I can't tell, it's all just heat and lust and craving, twisted tight inside me. I shake my head again, but he just smirks.

"Oh, I think you do. I think you're loving every minute of it... Shall we find out?"

He slips a hand under the waistband of my jeans. *Fuck.* My cheeks burn, and I try to twist away, but he holds me in a punishing grip as his fingers slide between my legs and dip into my wet heat.

I can't hide it; I'm dripping for him.

Sebastian hisses in satisfaction. "You can say I'm a monster, but you're the one getting drenched for me. So what does that make you?"

A liar. A fraud.

A traitor.

The words blur in my mind as Sebastian yanks my jeans all the way down, and then casually takes the half-empty wine bottle from the piano. "This is a 1990 Grand Cru," he announces, taking a gulp. I stare at him dumbly, still panting. He's talking about wine right now? "Twenty thousand pounds a bottle. But I bet it can taste a little sweeter, don't you think?"

Sebastian moves the bottle between my legs, and I gasp in

shock as the cool glass lip presses against my hot, aching flesh. "Wait," I gulp, reeling. There's no way he's going to...

But he does.

Sebastian slowly thrusts the bottle neck up into me.

Oh my God.

I grip onto him in disbelief, feeling the foreign glide of the smooth glass push inside. My mouth is open, but I can't even find the words for the whirlwind of emotions I'm feeling right now as Sebastian eases the bottle neck deeper inside me. I'm shocked, and humiliated...

And impossibly turned on.

And maybe I don't need to say a word. Maybe it's written all over my face, because Sebastian sounds a cruel laugh, watching me come undone. Obediently accepting everything he's giving me, my body yielding to the thick intrusion without protest.

"That's right, my Little Sparrow." he growls, almost mocking. "Open wide for Daddy. You can take it."

He brushes his thumb over my clit as the bottle neck twists inside me. I can't help sounding a cry of pleasure, but the desperate, needy sound is swallowed by his kiss. Cruel and dominating. Demanding my submission.

Still, I fight. I have to. I don't want to admit what he's saying is true, so I try to pull away, twist free from his iron-like grip.

Sebastian just fucks me with the bottle, withdrawing it a little, then thrusting it back inside, deeper than ever, the widening curve of the bottle neck stretching me open even thicker than his fingers have gone before.

Oh God.

I stifle a moan. A shudder of pleasure rolls through me, thick and sweet, even as I try to deny it.

I can't like this, I can't.

But I do.

The shock and humiliation just spur my pleasure on. Sebastian grips my hair painfully, yanking my head back so he can gorge on my throat, the bottle neck pumping thick inside me, stretching me out, as he grinds his palm against my clit.

"Look at you. Taking whatever I give you like a good fucking girl." Sebastian growls, thrusting deeper. "Because you *love* the monster inside me. Almost as much as you'll love it inside of you."

I cry out, but I refuse to give him what he wants from me.

I refuse to admit the truth.

"No," I sob, even as my climax starts to gather, sweet as poison in my toes.

"Yes." Sebastian suddenly slows, the bottle neck barely moving inside me. "Admit it. Now."

Fuck. I try to arch my hips, seeking out more friction, but he easily stops me, pinning me in place. I let out a desperate groan.

"If you want it, beg for it," Sebastian demands. "Beg this monster to get you off. Beg me to give this sweet cunt what it's craving."

No.

I feel tears of shame prick in the corner of my eyes. How can he do this to me? Strip back my defenses, and leave me gasping, despite all my rage and pain?

I don't want to want him. I don't want to need him.

But here I am, sobbing on the edge of a twisted, filthy climax only he could bring me to.

Only he can satiate.

"Or maybe you'd prefer to go to bed unsatisfied..." Sebastian makes to withdraw the bottle, leaving me empty and aching—

"No!" I cry in protest, and he stops.

Smiling.

Victorious.

"Use your words, Sparrow," he tells me, teasing the bottle around my clenching cunt. Dipping inside, making me grip for more. *Fuck.* "And make them good."

"Please," I cry, desperate.

"Please what?" he asks, his voice smooth as velvet.

God, I hate him. But I hate myself more.

"Please make me come," I whimper, grinding and clenching against him. The floodgates are open, and I'm mindless now, babbling. "Please," I beg, not caring how desperate I sound.

Because I am. That's the truth, isn't it? Sebastian's right. I want him, even like this. Whatever he does to me. Monster and all.

"I need it, please," I beg, clinging on to him. "I'll do anything, I'll be good for you, whatever you want. Just please, let me come, let me feel it, please!"

Sebastian looks at me with a cruel smile. "There you go," he growls, thrusting the bottle into me again, thick and deep. "You can't hide it, not from me. Because this monster knows exactly what you need, and I'll give it to you, every fucking time."

He twists it deeper, thicker. *Oh God.* "You're getting ready, baby," Sebastian growls, biting down on my earlobe. "You're almost ready for my cock. And I won't wait forever."

I groan at the idea, already struggling to take the bottle neck. It's impossibly thick now, stretching me out... almost too much to take—

My orgasm shatters me so fast, I don't even have time to scream. I'm just consumed by the ecstasy, spasming violently against his hand as the pleasure crashes through me.

And Sebastian doesn't stop. *Fuck.* He's still pumping into me, stroking my clit, keeping me right there on the edge until—

Oh my God.

I come again, harder this time, and I swear, my mind goes black, reeling from the shock of it all.

When I come back to my senses, Sebastian has released me. I'm sagged against the piano, as he slowly brings the bottle away from me and takes a sip.

"Delicious. You know, I think I like a little fight in you," he muses. "It makes it even sweeter when you finally submit."

I gasp for air, flushed with pleasure—and the crushing weight of self-loathing, already chasing my glow away.

What have you done?

My legs are weak, but somehow, I manage to straighten, and put one foot in front of the other, all the way to the door. I don't manage a witty parting shot, or any words at all. I don't even look at him as I walk out of the room, and slowly make my way up the stairs.

I can't let him be the one who walks away. Not this time. I'm too shaken by what just happened here. And the most disturbing part is how much I liked it.

Craved it.

He took what he wanted from me, without mercy, and still, I begged for more.

"Admit it, you like the monster..."

I shiver. It isn't true... Is it?

No. *It can't be.* I'm here to destroy the monster, not submit to him. This was just a momentary madness, I reassure myself desperately: The usual toxic cocktail of desire and vengeance, even if he pushed it so much further than ever before.

So much deeper.

I shudder with the memory of my climax, somehow more powerful than ever. I don't understand, the more he pushes my boundaries, the more extreme my body's reaction is. And tonight...

It was almost too much for me to take. In the best, most fucked-up ways.

I gulp, still reeling. I need to shower him off me. Try and wash the shame away. Even though I know, it runs deeper than that. I go turn the shower on, and strip my clothes off, exhausted. I'm just reaching for a robe, when I see something.

A brown manila envelope sitting on my bed.

I move closer, bracing myself for another twisted game from Sebastian, but my name is scrawled on the front in unfamiliar writing.

I tear it open. There's a photo inside, black and white, surveillance-style.

Of me.

This morning. I'm outside the library, talking to James beside the coffee cart. The photographer has captured us at the moment he was reaching to pick that lint from my hair.

It looks like he's caressing my cheek.

My heart pounds. I stare at the photo in disbelief.

Who took this? Someone was following me?

I check the envelope again, and a scrap of paper falls out. A handwritten note, with no name.

Does Sebastian know you're not as innocent as you seem?

Chapter 19

Avery

I barely sleep that night, and not because I'm still shaken by the intensity of my climax with Sebastian, pinned there against the piano he bought, just for me. My mind is spinning, and my body is wired, tight with this new, unthinkable threat.

Someone's been following me.

But who sent the photo? Why? Is it some kind of threat?

What do they want from me?

I briefly wonder if it's Sebastian's doing, keeping tabs, but I know that's not it. He wouldn't have watched me from a distance, taking photos like some kind of creepy paparazzi stalking a celebrity. It's not his style. He's direct—to a fault. Last night proved that beyond all question.

What about Becca? Those are almost the same words she said to me that morning:

"You're not as innocent as you seem..."

But what's her angle here? Is she trying to scare me away from Sebastian out of jealousy—or some twisted idea of protection?

My list of other suspects is frustratingly short. I don't know anybody else in London—and they wouldn't know me, either. I've been here a matter of weeks, and hardly met anyone, unless I'm out on Sebastian's arm. And even then, I'm not important enough to register, they're all just focused on getting to him. I'm the arm-candy, his latest flavor of the week. Nobody even thinks I'll last the month with him, so they wouldn't go out of their way to target me like this.

... Unless someone has discovered the truth about my real mission here.

That idea is even more chilling.

I thought I'd covered my tracks, but if they've seen me at the library, then they must know I'm not just out shopping all day. That I'm busy with a secret project—that involves tracking down any information I can about Sebastian and his company.

But if it is Becca who's discovered what I'm really doing here, and she wants to expose me, then why send the photos to me? Surely she would just take that information straight to Sebastian, and have him confront me instead.

No... The stalker-style photo, the anonymous note. It feels like a warning... But why?

I puzzle over it from every angle, but by the time morning finally dawns, I'm no closer to figuring out what's going on.

Whatever the truth is, one thing is clear: I'm running out of time.

I've been lulled into a kind of routine here the past week, a twisted kind of normalcy. By day, I carry out my research, learning more about Sebastian and his business dealings. And by night... I learn a whole different kind of lesson, as he masterfully pushes my body to breaking point, showing me a pleasure that I never dreamed possible.

And can't forgive myself for enjoying.

It's a routine, a seductive rhythm I've settled into, but now that has to change. And not just because last night's lesson has shaken me to the core, and shown me a glimpse of something inside me I don't want to see. If my cover could be blown at any minute, I need to shift gears—and fast. No more library research, fact-finding missions, no more loitering around the house, hoping to sneak a look in locked rooms and private drawers.

No more begging for him, as he strips away my defenses and leaves me sobbing with pleasure.

I've been *reacting* to Sebastian. Letting him set the terms of this arrangement. Playing along with his games and biding my time.

Now, I need to move into the attack. Before he shows me a side of myself that I can't take back.

And I know exactly where to start: the mysterious address in Sussex, where Sebastian has stashed away some kind of secret.

It's time to bring those dark secrets into the light.

First thing in the morning, I'm out the door, with a breezy mention of a luxurious spa day. Sebastian is already gone, thankfully, so I just chatter to Leon and the driver, about the miraculous mud wraps and divine pedicures I have lined up. I even go inside the health club when the driver drops me off, just to sell the story, before waiting ten minutes, and sneaking out a side entrance.

If Sebastian knew where I was going today, he'd probably chain me up in the wine cellar. But knowing somebody is watching me, waiting to make their move...

I need to make mine first.

I take a taxi to Victoria Station. At the library, I already figured out the route closest to the address, so it's pretty straightforward to buy a ticket from the machine—plus another burner phone from a news kiosk. I find the right platform and get settled on the train. At this time of day, the carriages are quiet, and I find an empty spot with nobody around. As the train pulls away, winding slowly through South London, I begin to set up the phone.

I call Nero, knowing it's been a while since I checked in. His wife, Lily, answers on the first ring.

"It's me," I say, and I can hear the relief in her voice when she replies.

"Thank God. We've been so worried."

"I'm fine," I lie, not wanting to worry her. "Remember, you're the society princess, I'm the badass and indestructible one."

She snorts with laughter. Lily is anything but a princess, she's the only woman I know who could keep Nero in line, for starters. "Is it terrible, playing along with Sebastian?" she asks, sounding concerned. "I can't imagine, having to smile at that man. To kiss him, and... you know." she tactfully trails off.

I feel a rush of guilt. Here Lily is, thinking I'm in hell, when every night, I come screaming Sebastian's name.

"I'll be glad when it's over," I tell her honestly. I hear Nero's voice in the background, and then he takes the phone.

"What do you need?"

I smile. Nero knows this would never just be a social call.

"The hacker you used, to set up my fake identity," I say, glancing around to make sure nobody is close enough to overhear. "Are they good?"

"The best," Nero replies confidently.

"So, would they be able to move money between accounts, out of Wolfe Capital?" I ask.

"Shouldn't be a problem. But you should know, a company like that will flag the transactions, they keep shit locked up tight over there. Otherwise, I would have drained those fuckers dry a long time ago," Nero adds darkly.

"It's OK," I reassure him. "I want the transactions to be found. It should look like embezzlement, that they've been siphoning off funds for a while."

Nero whistles. "Who got on your bad side?"

"Her name's Rebecca Hargreaves, she's a senior VP over there. Have your hacker make it look good, only take from accounts she would have a chance of accessing."

"Consider it done," Nero replies. "Does this mean you're any closer to coming home?"

Home. It sounds like a foreign word to me now.

"Not until Wolfe is buried," I reply. "Talk soon."

I hang up before he can say another word. Setting up Becca without any proof that she's a threat to me might be extreme, but I can't risk her blowing my cover and getting in my way.

I feel a twinge of guilt but push it aside. *You need to be heartless, remember?* And Becca is no innocent, caught in the crossfire. She's a grown woman who's chosen her path in life and being the right-hand woman to Sebastian Wolfe for the past decade means she's got plenty of blood on her hands.

She suspects me of having a secret agenda, she's made that clear. That makes her a threat. And if she really is the one who sent that photo to threaten me?

Either way, my problem will soon be solved.

Two hours on the train and another taxi ride later, I arrive in the small village of Hartley Wells, which is right out of a picture postcard: charming village green, small stores, a local pub... The house Sebastian has been paying for is a few miles past the village, on a winding country road with no neighbors to be seen. It's a pretty cottage, set back from the road down a winding path, but still, I feel a flicker of trepidation as the taxi drives away, leaving me alone. It's a cloudy, overcast day, and I'm in the middle of nowhere, about to walk into who knows what.

Just what is Sebastian hiding away out here?

It could be a secret family, an illegitimate child... or something far more dangerous. I'm taking a huge risk just showing up like this, but I remember what brought me here, and why.

Vengeance.

I have to be as ruthless as Sebastian if I'm going to destroy him. There's no room for fear and emotion.

Or desire...

I shake off that unwelcome thought and approach the front door. Bracing myself for what may be behind it, I knock.

There's silence.

I try again, louder.

Still nothing.

Hoping that this hasn't all been a waste of time, I skirt around the house, peering in windows. I see pretty, country-style furnishings, but no sign of life inside, so I unlatch the gate and step into the backyard. I can see here that the house backs onto open fields, with some stables a short distance away.

There's a woman there, grooming one of the horses.

This is it.

I take a deep breath and approach her. She's so focused on her task, she doesn't notice me coming closer, and I have plenty of time to take her in.

She's young, in her late twenties maybe, with dark hair in a braid, and dressed down in muddy boots and an oversized knit sweater.

My boots squelch in a puddle, and she jumps, turning. "You scared me!"

"I'm sorry," I say quickly.

"Can I help you?" the woman asks, looking at me warily.

"Umm..." My mind is blank, and I realize, I don't have much of a game plan now that I'm here. I didn't know what to expect, so I couldn't really prepare.

So, I go direct. "I need to talk to you about Sebastian Wolfe."

In an instant, the wary look is replaced with a wry smile. The woman laughs, patting the horse. "What's my brother done now?"

I blink at her in shock.

"Brother?" I echo, my mind reeling.

"I'm his little sister." She wipes off her hand, and holds it out to shake, smiling brightly. "Scarlett Wolfe."

Chapter 20

Avery

Sebastian's sister isn't dead.

I can't believe it.

Scarlett invites me in for tea, and I follow her to the house, my mind racing. I go back over our conversations, the way he talked about her in the past tense, went along with me when I assumed she'd passed away...

But he never said that she'd died.

So why don't I know about her? Why was there no mention of her in any of the articles I read about his family?

Hell, why didn't his mother ever mention her during our visit to the country?

"How do you take your tea?"

I blink. Scarlett is fixing the drinks for us in her warm, comfortable kitchen, while I sit at the big farmhouse table, trying to put the whole story together. "Umm, however you like it is fine." I say, watching her curiously. Now I know what to look for, I can see the resemblance to Sebastian in their jawline, and the way her dark hair frames her face.

"Are you sure about that?" she asks, teasing. "Seb always

says I take it with enough sugar to start a sweet shop. He, of course, sticks to coffee. Black, like his heart," she adds with a wink.

I manage a nervous laugh. "He took cream once, when he thought I wasn't looking," I find myself saying. "Then swore he was fixing it for me."

Scarlett brightens. "So, you're dating him, then?"

I cough. Dating is hardly the word I'd use to describe our twisted arrangement, but I'm not about to go into that with her now. I'm the one with questions, and I want answers.

"We're seeing each other, yes," I finally reply. "And I'm sorry to drop by like this. He... doesn't really mention you," I add. "And I was... Curious."

Understatement of the year.

Scarlett gives me a casual shrug, bringing our tea over to the table. "Well, there's really no big mystery. I prefer a quieter life, so I keep to myself out here, with the horses. All those society events, all the attention Sebastian gets in the city... It's not my thing," she finishes. "Give me a muddy paddock over a VIP list any day."

I smile along with her, but something's still not adding up. Wanting a quiet life is one thing, but your entire family acting like you're dead?

There's more to the story here.

I decide to do some more gentle digging. "I can see why you like it here," I say, sitting back, and looking around. "It's so pretty, the open fields. You can really breathe."

"Exactly." Scarlett smiles. "Plus, the horses wouldn't be happy in the city. They like a good hack in the hills."

"So you've been here a while?" I ask casually, taking a sip of my tea.

Scarlett nods. "How about some biscuits?" she says getting to her feet again.

"Sure." I watch her bustle in the kitchen cupboards. She seems a little nervous under the surface, even if she's trying to play it cool. "It must get a little lonely, being so far from everyone."

"I like it that way."

"Still, at your age, you must want to meet people. Did you go to college at Oxford, like your brother?"

"No."

"That's right, my mistake," I watch her carefully. "That's when you would have been at Larkspur."

I'm taking a wild guess here, dropping the name of the psychiatric hospital I found in the file, but I know I've hit the bullseye when all the color drains from her face.

Scarlett's mug falls to the floor, shattering on the tile.

Shit.

"I'm sorry," I blurt, quickly rushing to help her. Scarlett recoils from me, her eyes wide and panicked. "It's OK," I tell her, already feeling bad for scaring her.

Whatever happened with this Larkspur place, it clearly wasn't sunshine and roses if just the mention of the name makes her react like this.

"I've got it, don't cut yourself," I tell her, clearing up the broken pieces. I find a cloth and wipe up the spilled tea. "There, good as new."

But Scarlett doesn't look good. She sinks into a chair, clearly trying to regulate her breathing.

"Are you OK?" I ask, concerned.

Slowly, she takes another breath, and nods. "I'm fine. Really," she adds, clocking my concerned gaze. "Except for breaking my favorite mug. I'm so clumsy sometimes," she gives me a fake smile, and gets to her feet, going to fix another mug of tea.

I watch her, feeling like the worst person in the world. Especially because I know, I can't stop digging now.

"So, Larkspur..." I prompt, hating myself—but not enough to bite my tongue. Whatever Sebastian and Scarlett have been hiding here, I need to know.

Scarlett brushes back her hair. "It's not a big deal," she says, even though all her behavior would say otherwise. "After the crash, I had some... Difficulties."

Wait, the crash...?

I stare at her, wide-eyed. "You were there, in the car with—"

"With my father, yes." Scarlett nods. "The night he died. I was twelve."

She pushes up her sleeves in a nervous gesture, and it's only then that I see the pale scarring on her arms: mottled tissue, like she's been burned.

Scarlett sees me looking and tugs her sleeves back down again. "As you can imagine, it wasn't a great time for me," she continues quietly. "Afterwards... Well, I struggled. But I'm fine now. Because of Sebastian. My brother's always taken care of me," she says, sounding firmer now. "He's the best, but you must know that by now," she adds with a smile—genuine, this time. "He takes care of everything."

I flush. That much is true, but I'm guessing we're thinking about very different versions of Sebastian Wolfe. To me, that care has been dominant and merciless. I can't believe there might be a different side to him, not matter what his sister is telling me.

His sister...

I'm about to ask her more when I hear a loud whirring noise overhead. Through the kitchen window, I can see a helicopter approaching, a dark speck on the horizon roaring closer.

Scarlett laughs. "Uh oh. We're in trouble now," she says, but her tone is light and teasing. "He only takes the chopper when he's extra-mad about something."

Sebastian.

Scarlett doesn't seem worried, she's eagerly pulling on her jacket and rushing out to meet the helicopter as it lands, but I hang back, dread pooling in the pit of my stomach.

If he knows I'm here... How much more does he know?

And what kind of punishment will I get for the crime of my curiosity?

I step outside, watching as he emerges from the helicopter, dressed for business, as if he just flew in from a meeting. Which, he probably did.

Even from a distance, I can see the fury clear on his face. He stalks toward us, tension in the lines of his body and a deep frown on his face.

"Seb!" Scarlett greets him with a hug. Sebastian hugs her back, but only briefly. He pulls away. "You're supposed to call me if anyone comes," he tells her, shooting his icy gaze my way for just a moment before refocusing on her. "You just invited her in?"

Scarlett rolls her eyes, and even though she's older than me, she seems so much younger in the way she playfully pushes Sebastian. "Of course I did. I'm not all surly and suspicious like you. And anyway, I figured one of your security team would get the message to you. That's what all the cameras are for, right?"

Cameras. Of course. Why didn't I think of that? No wonder Sebastian made it here so fast, I probably triggered some kind of alarm the moment I stepped foot on the property.

Sloppy, Avery, I scold myself, as Sebastian's gaze burns into me. I'm expecting him to start yelling any second now, but instead, he restrains his temper—for Scarlett.

"You still should've called," he chides her, but his tone his gentle. Scarlett giggles.

"You're going to get frown lines, with all your brooding,"

she teases him. "And then all the money in the world won't stop you looking like Yoda."

Sebastian shakes his head, softening. "Sure it will. Haven't you heard of a little thing called Botox?" he shoots back, playful.

Scarlett hoots with laughter. "If you get Botox, I'm never letting you hear the end of it," she says, gleeful. "You saw what it did to mum when she tried it. She couldn't frown for a month! Just walked around looking mildly puzzled at everything."

"That makes a change from her usual pinot-fueled stupor." Sebastian replies, with a wry grin.

I stare at the two of them in shock as they playfully banter and joke around. Who the hell is this, and what has he done with the real Sebastian Wolfe?

I'm wondering if this is some sophisticated AI, when Sebastian fixes me with an icy glare that chills me to the core.

"We're leaving. Get in the chopper," he orders me.

Nope, same old Sebastian.

"You're leaving already?" Scarlett pouts. "Stay, for dinner at least. I want to get to know Avery. And tell her embarrassing stories about you, and a certain goth phase..."

"Another time," Sebastian cuts her off. "But I'll see you this weekend."

"And Avery?" Scarlett asks hopefully.

Sebastian's jaw clenches. "Avery's busy. Aren't you." His eyes bore into me.

"Sorry," I blurt, already wondering if I'll be in the country by the weekend, based on the subtle fury radiating from his every glance and move. "But it was lovely meeting you," I add. "And thanks for the tea."

Scarlett says goodbye, and Sebastian stalks back to the helicopter. I grab my things and follow, my heart pounding with dread. I glance around, seriously contemplating making a run for it. But I know I wouldn't get far.

Sebastian would probably just chase me down himself.

There's nothing for it. I have to face the music—and hope I can cover enough to keep him off my scent.

I climb inside the helicopter, buckling into the seat beside him. Thankfully, the moment the engine starts again, the noise is deafening. Even with a headset on, there's no chance of talking, so we spend the trip back to London in silence, as I'm slowly consumed with a chilling sense of doom.

How can I explain this to him?

I have no idea where to even begin. And even though I should be desperately wracking my brains for a cover story for my little field trip, all I can do is replay the events of the day.

Who is the caring brother Scarlett described, the one I just saw tease and banter with her? Everything I've known of Sebastian so far is heartless and uncompromising. Since the day we met, he's barely shown a glimpse of humanity. In fact, he seems to take pleasure in proving his dominance, making me weak.

Making me beg.

And before that... Well, I know his crimes. I've seen the damage he's done, without a hint of remorse.

He said it himself last night: he's a monster. Irredeemable.

I glance over at him, stone-faced beside me. It's clear, whatever softness he shows his sister, it certainly doesn't apply to me. He's on a knife-edge, full of rage that's about to be unleashed in one direction.

Me.

I shiver. I need to tread carefully, if I'm going to survive the night with my cover story intact. Because who knows how far Sebastian will go to punish the ones who wrong him?

This is not a forgiving man.

And when we land in London, and are whisked to his waiting car, I see that for myself, up close.

His phone rings as soon as we get into the backseat. He answers, impatient. "What?"

He listens for a moment, then shakes his head. "No, you must be mistaken. Becca wouldn't be so foolish."

I remember what I asked Nero to do, setting up a trail of embezzlement that leads right back to Becca. Clearly, his hacker works fast.

"You're certain?" Sebastian listens for another minute, his features hardening. When he speaks, his voice is so cold that I feel a trickle of fear just from the sound of it.

"Then she's done. Freeze her assets, cut off her access. I want an example made of her. And no, don't file charges with the police, I'll handle it myself," he adds, with a chilling smile. "The law is nothing compared to the hell I'm about to rain down on that thieving bitch."

He hangs up.

Ten years of loyalty clearly means nothing to the man; Becca is done at Wolfe Capital.

I take a deep breath. I should be happy, that's one problem solved.

But I know it won't help me now.

When we reach the house, the place is dark and empty. The staff have clearly all been sent home, which worries me even more. Did he have them leave because he doesn't want witnesses here?

Just what it is he capable of?

Sebastian strolls to the living room and pours himself a drink at the bar. I trail behind him, on edge. Waiting for the explosion I know is coming.

He's standing next to the beautiful piano when he finally turns to me and speaks.

"What the fuck are you playing at?" he asks. His gaze searches me, and I'm surprised to find confusion in his usually superior gaze.

He doesn't know the truth.

Relief washes through me, so intense I almost sink to the floor. My secret agenda is still safe. Sebastian doesn't understand that I'm trying to destroy him. He doesn't see what I was really up to with my trip to Sussex.

Which means I have a way to talk myself out of this. *God.* I take a deep breath, my mind racing. This is my only chance, and I have to deliver the performance of a lifetime.

"I'm sorry," I say, making my voice small. I try to sound like I'm on the verge of tears, which doesn't take much, after the rollercoaster of emotions I've gone through today. "I shouldn't have gone to find Scarlett."

"So why did you?" Sebastian's eyes drill into me. He's wary, on-edge, and I know, the smallest misstep will send him into a furious rage.

And for good reason. Because if he knew what I was really doing...

I gulp, not needing to fake my anxiety or fear in this moment. "I just... I want to know you!" I exclaim, taking a step towards him. "I've been here for weeks, and sometimes, it's like we're getting closer, but then... You push me away and keep these walls up around you. You have all these secrets," I add, keeping my eyes wide and plaintive. "You won't let me in, and I just... I just wanted to know more, that's all."

I sound desperate and needy. Good. He has to feel like he has all the power right now, that I'm just a weak, smitten girl wanting to be closer to him.

"You don't understand what it's been like," I continue, my

voice shaking with emotion. "You just whisked me away from everything I know, you saved me from Nero, and it's been this incredible whirlwind, but I thought... I thought it wouldn't mean anything to me. But it does." I take another step closer. "*You* do. I didn't expect any of this, but I can't control how I'm feeling. All these emotions, the things you do to me..."

I trail off, as if I'm overwhelmed. And I am. Because the truth is, my words aren't entirely a lie.

I didn't expect any of this. I can't control how I'm feeling, how much I want him, and the twisted, fucked-up things we do in the dark.

How his lessons are unravelling me, and everything I thought I knew about myself.

And maybe it's that kernel of truth that's my saving grace, because Sebastian takes a long, slow swallow of whiskey...

And then exhales. Relaxing.

"You could have just asked me," he says, looking weary. "Instead of disturbing my sister like that."

He bought it.

Holy shit. I try not to show my relief. "I *have* asked you, all kinds of things," I say, moving closer. "But you just deflect everything personal about your life. Why won't you open up?" I gaze up at him. "I just want to know you. To *understand* you."

Sebastian gives me a ghost of a smile. Full of bitterness, and something else too, something dark I can't quite decipher. "Are you sure about that?"

"Yes." I say, closing the distance between us. I take his hand, and gently guide him to the couch. I can't believe it, but I almost feel like his defenses are coming down.

"What did Scarlett tell you?" Sebastian asks, looking down at where I'm still holding his hand.

I take a careful breath. "She said that she was in the car accident that killed your father," I venture gently. "That she had some... problems after, and that you take care of her. She loves you very much," I add. "Says you're the best brother in the world."

Sebastian gives a short laugh, but instead of the usual sarcasm in his tone, this one sounds almost sad. "Scarlett was always a troubled kid," he begins quietly. "Even before the accident. We went through a dozen diagnoses, had her in therapy, and medication... But it got worse after what happened. And not just the trauma of losing dad. She was badly hurt in the crash. Burned."

I think back to the burn marks on her arms and answer sincerely. "I'm sorry, that's awful."

Sebastian drains his drink. "She survived the crash, but everything spiraled after that. Breakdowns, episodes... Whatever you want to call them. She tried to hurt herself, I tried everything, but... Richard suggested Larkspur. He said it was the best facility around, it would give her the help she needed, and mum went along with it, she was at her wit's end too. But that place..." Sebastian's gaze darkens. "It's a hellhole. They drugged her up, kept her locked in her room, did all kinds of things to the patients... The first time I was allowed to visit, she begged me to get her out. And I tried. I really did. But I had no rights, I was only eighteen, mum was the only one with legal authority, and Richard was whispering in her ear..."

Sebastian looks at me, his expression full of broken remorse. "I failed her," he says, his voice cracking at the memory. "It took two years until I inherited the trust, and I could get her out of there. Two years, she spent in that place. In hell. And after, trying to get her to heal from what they put her through..."

I squeeze his hand instinctively. "But you did it," I tell him, my heart in my throat. "You got her out. She seems happy now."

He nods slowly, but the ache in his eyes doesn't go away. "I was willing to do anything. I found her the best therapists, the right medication. The horses were the big breakthrough, equine therapy. It sounded like hippie nonsense to me," he adds with a wry look, "but whatever the fuck it took. And I finally had the resources to make it happen. Richard threw a fit, but he couldn't do anything. I had the company. Wolfe Capital. I finally could call the shots. You see, money... It buys you everything. Even protection from the shadows hiding under the bed."

"So the cameras, the security at the house... It's for Scarlett's sake, too," I say, realizing.

He nods. "She's come a long way, but a part of her is still terrified that Larkspur will come and drag her back to that place again. I've told her she can come and live with me," he adds, "But she wants to try and be independent. It means a lot to her, to be able to live on her own terms now."

"And you made that happen," I say, moved, despite everything. I never thought Sebastian was capable of real love, but his devotion to his sister is plain to see. "You take care of her."

"Not enough." He shakes his head, that dark expression in his eyes again. "Not nearly enough to make up for any of it."

I wonder what he means by that, but before I can say anything, Sebastian pulls his hand away from mine. "There," he says, looking closed off again, "You wanted to know me, well, there it is. Enough for you yet?"

"No."

My answer slips from my lips before I can stop it. "No, not enough," I say, and before I can stop myself, I'm reaching up and pulling his face down to mine.

I kiss him.

It's the first time, I realize, when our lips meet in a rush of slow, tender heat. The first time I've been the one reaching for him, pursuing him, instead of receiving his passion. Now, I press my lips to his, searching, my hands moving to tangle his hair as his mouth parts, and my tongue slides against his.

Sebastian sounds a low groan. His hands close around my waist, pulling me into his lap as our tongues tangle in a sensual dance.

God yes... It's wrong, every rational part of me is screaming at this betrayal, but fuck, it feels too good in his arms. I'm acting on pure instinct now, I couldn't stop it if I tried. I arch up against him, eagerly exploring his mouth, my body already aching to draw him closer and anchor myself to him.

Where I belong.

The unwanted thought shocks me out of the moment, and I start to pull away, but Sebastian is gripping me tightly now, deepening the kiss, something animal and desperate in his movements. It's overwhelming, intense, and I feel myself slip into the undertow, desire snaking through me, binding me to him.

I'm gasping when he finally breaks the kiss. Sebastian looks down at me, and the raw heat in his eyes takes my breath away.

"I'm done waiting," he says, voice thick with lust. "It's time for your final lesson, Sparrow. I'm taking what's mine."

Chapter 21

Avery

This is it...

I follow Sebastian upstairs, my heart pounding in my chest. I always imagined my first time would be with Miles. That it would be something tender and sweet, full of real emotion. It would matter because we were meant to be together.

Instead, I'm trading my innocence for revenge.

But I want it, too.

I can't deny it, not when anticipation is already curling in my veins. Not when I'm wet for him, thighs clenching with every step, aching to feel him inside me.

I can't explain it, the physical hold he has over me. This toxic chemistry that draws me closer, even as my mind—and heart—scream at me to stay away. It doesn't make any sense, but my body has been primed for this since the very first time he kissed me. The way my body has come alive under his expert hands and wicked tongue...

I'm not so naïve that I can't see that he planned it this way: Drawing me in, tempting me with pleasure, guiding me lesson by sinful lesson to this very moment as I follow him up the stairs and down the hall to his bedroom.

Every sensual touch and thrilling climax has driven me closer and closer to the edge. And now...

Now, despite everything, I find myself longing for the freefall.

Sebastian's suite is as sparsely decorated as the rest of the house, dominated by a king-sized bed covered with crisp linens. Lamps cast the room in a dim glow.

He closes the door behind us. "Come here," he says, beckoning me to meet him by the bed.

I go to him, my heart pounding so loudly in my chest, I'm sure he can hear it.

Sebastian's eyes sweep over me, satisfied. "Are you nervous?"

I shake my head automatically, but the smile playing on his lips tells me that he knows the truth.

"Don't be. Arms up," Sebastian instructs me, and I do as he says. Slowly, he strips my shirt over my head. "You see, this was inevitable. From the moment I saw you at the poker table, I knew, you'd wind up here. In my bed. There was no other outcome on the table."

"That's pretty arrogant," I find my voice, and he smiles, his gaze pouring over my body like the fine whiskey he drinks: slow and sweet, and burning me all the way down.

"You don't understand, my sweet. When I want something... I won't stop until it's mine." He trails his fingertips over my collarbone, making me shiver.

Making me ache.

Sebastian circles me, leaning in, to murmur in my ear. "I knew I'd break you."

Anger flashes in my bloodstream, but before I can object, my bra falls away, leaving me half-naked and exposed. My hands come up to cover myself, but Sebastian takes my wrists in one hand, pinning them behind my back.

"You can't hide from me now, Sparrow," he murmurs, "I've waited so patiently for this moment." He cups my chin and brings his face so close to mine that I can see the intensity blazing in his eyes. "Now, tell me 'Yes.' Tell me you want this. Beg for my cock."

I clench my jaw closed. Even now, at the last moment, when surrender seems inevitable, a part of me is still trying to hold back. To keep myself from him.

Remember why I'm really here.

"Say it," Sebastian orders me, seductively soft. "I told you once, I won't ever force a woman." His hands trail over my half-naked body, casually sending shivers of pleasure racing through me. "So, either give yourself to me willingly now... Or leave, tonight, and never come back."

There's no choice here. My body has already decided for me.

And my heart...

My heart is still set on having its revenge.

"Yes."

My voice comes out a whisper. It cuts me like a betrayal.

"Yes, what?" Sebastian inhales, a sharp breath of anticipation.

"Yes... I belong to you," I tell him, my voice shaking. "I want... I want you. All of it. *Show me.*"

Sebastian hisses with satisfaction. "That's my good girl," he murmurs, and my knees go weak. "I'll take care of you. I promise..."

I wait eagerly for oblivion, for the ruthless dominance I know will sweep me up in sensation and blot all these doubts and guilty feelings from my mind.

But Sebastian doesn't pounce or grab me roughly. With

steady hands, he strips my jeans down, and then goes down on his knees to peel my panties off, guiding my legs out of the silky scrap, breath hot on my stomach.

"Look at you..." he growls, "So beautiful. So fucking wet for me."

No.

I sway, feeling dizzy with desperation. I don't want him to seduce me. I don't want gentle, tender words.

I need this to be over with, before...

Before I want it to last.

"Sebastian—" I start, reaching for him, but he ignores my breathless plea.

"The most precious prize is always worth the wait." Sebastian teases, nudging my thighs. I part them for him immediately, and he chuckles, seeing how eagerly my body responds to his touch. "That's right, you know who owns your pleasure now."

He turns my body one way, and the other, admiring me, like he's testing my pliant resolve. "Are you sure you don't want to protest, the way you always do, pretending as you don't want this? Like you're not tight and dripping, hungry for my cock."

His voice is thick with victory, but I can't lie—not to myself, not anymore. *I want him.* My body aches for him. And maybe, maybe once he claims me, it will break this fever. Free me from the torment of this cruel desire.

The thought takes bloom in my mind, offering me a last gasp of hope in the midst of this dark seduction.

Isn't that how ancient medicines always worked? A taste of the poison is the cure. So perhaps once tonight is over, and I know the thick thrust of his cock inside me, I'll be free from wanting him.

It's my only hope.

I thrust forward, into his hands. "You said this was my final lesson," I tell him, my heart racing with a new determination. "So teach me," I demand. *"Take me.* Tell me what to do."

"Oh, don't you worry... I will." Sebastian straightens, stripping off his clothes. I realize, I've never seen him naked. Never even seen him without his shirt on.

Now, I drink in the sight of him. His broad shoulders, the taut, packed muscle of his torso. The trail of dark hair, leading down his stomach to—

His cock.

Thick and stiff, jutting from his body. Bigger than anything I've taken before. I feel a shudder of anticipation.

"You're my prize. I'm going to enjoy you."

He lays me back on the bed, in total control. I suck in a gasp, bracing myself, but still, Sebastian holds back, his hands gliding softly over my body, his mouth grazing over my skin. He licks up the inside of my thigh... Caresses my bare breasts... Trails his tongue across my stomach... Every new movement brings a rush of awareness, my nerves sparking like wildfire, until my entire body is lit up, trembling, aching for more.

Damn him.

I can feel my resolve slip, the protective barrier around my emotions start to crack, with every slow, sensual caress. I could take it hard. Keep the distance if he was rough and cruel with me. But Sebastian is coaxing an unwelcome haze of pleasure from my body. His fingers slide down my torso, but he barely skims between my legs, brushing over my clit. He won't stay where I need, won't give me the pleasure of any friction or pressure, and it doesn't take long before I'm whimpering with need.

"Sebastian..." I gasp, clutching the sheets.

"Yes, my sweet?" he's poised above me, eyes dark, watching every sob and moan with a look of fevered satisfaction on his face.

"I need... I need..."

"A good fuck," Sebastian finishes for me. I flush at his crude words, and he chuckles. "Still the innocent... Don't worry. You won't be blushing after you come, clenching all over my cock. When you beg me to fuck you deeper, because you're starving for just one more inch." He leans over, his hand resting softly on my throat. "You'll be a good little whore for me, won't you, Sparrow?"

Fuck.

His honeyed words unlock something deep inside me, and a moan sounds, in a voice I don't even recognize as I shudder in delight.

"Yes... Oh God, *Please.*"

"That's it." Sebastian croons. He takes a condom from the nightstand and rolls it on his thick length. "That's what you want, isn't it?" He pulls me down the bed until I'm at the very edge of it, then positions himself between my legs. He grips my thighs, easing me open me to him, his cockhead pressing, blunt at my entrance.

"Now, be a good girl, and take it all."

He thrusts inside me, sinfully slow.

Oh fuck. My jaw drops in a silent scream, as the size of him splits me open. He's big, too big, stretching me open even though his cock is barely nudging inside—*too much.* All of it, I can't—

"Yes you can," Sebastian hushes me, inching deeper. "Look at me, Sparrow. Let me in."

He reaches down and presses a palm to my cheek. Our eyes lock, and *God*, the intimacy sends a shudder through me. *Opening me to him.* "Fuck, yes, just like that. You're taking me so well," he groans in satisfaction, "So tight for me, so sweet. Such a good fucking girl."

The glow of his praise rolls through me, unlocking something deep inside. Sebastian sinks into me again, even deeper this time.

"Fuck," he hisses, and I have to gasp for air, shocked by the way his cock feels embedded inside me, stretching me.

I'm filled, pinned, totally possessed.

And god, it feels so fucking good.

Sebastian must see the wonder on my face, because he leans over, and presses a tender kiss to my forehead. "I'm just getting started, sweetheart," he promises me, his breath ragged with self-control. "I'm going to make you feel so good. This sweet cunt is made to take me. You feel that?"

He takes my hand, and presses it to my lower abdomen, so I can feel the thick bulge of him deep inside. I shiver with awareness.

"This is the cock that owns you now." Sebastian presses my hand harder, as he slowly withdraws an inch or two, and sinks in again, even deeper. "This is the cock that's going to make you beg and scream."

Holy shit. I moan, as an unfamiliar pleasure ripples through me. I wriggle against him, clenching, *wanting.*

Sebastian chuckles. "Already hungry for more?"

I pant, writhing, flushed with sensation.

"Don't worry, my darling. I'll give you everything you need."

He sinks into me again, exquisitely slowly, his dark gaze still locked on mine. The rock of his body is incredible, pleasure suffusing every part of me as I feel my body blossom, matching his movements, opening up to him.

To the tenderness in his eyes, and the soft caress of his hands skimming over my skin.

I melt, falling into the bliss of it all, reaching up blindly to pull his face closer and claim his lips in a hot, desperate kiss. Our tongues tangle, as his cock surges inside me, and God, it's everything, the connection like nothing else. Something shimmering, and raw, and real, as our bodies rock together, and I feel myself falling, clinging onto him, never wanting to let go ...

No.

I gasp for air. Wracked with sudden shame as my mind races.

What am I doing?

Sebastian is still slowly thrusting into me, whispering praise and platitudes in my ear. How beautiful I am. How well I'm taking him. Soft, and gentle, and full of a new tenderness that makes my body shudder and gasp beneath him.

And my heart melts, wanting more.

I can't fall for this man. *I won't.*

"More," I demand breathlessly, surging up against him. "Take me harder."

Concern flashes on Sebastian's face. "I don't want to hurt you."

Damn it.

Hurt would be better than this sweetness. Pain would drown out my guilt and shame. Sebastian's tenderness isn't enough. I can still think, still hate myself for wanting this, still feel the sharp bite of self-loathing for giving myself to him.

I wrap my legs around his hips. My eyes burn into his. "You're holding back," I groan, arching against him. "Don't. Show me the monster. You know I want it, too. You know what I *need.*"

Sebastian's eyes flash with shock—and then hot, determined lust. He sounds a groan. "Fuck, Sparrow, don't tempt me..."

I grind down, and clench my inner muscles, milking his cock.

"Teach me," I hiss, scratching my nails down his back. "Take me. Make me your good little whore."

Sebastian breaks. With a roar, he pulls back, and then slams into me. Hard.

I cry out, jolting with the thick impact, but he doesn't pause for a second, Sebastian pins me down, and fucks me to the hilt. Over and over. Merciless.

"Is this how you like it, Sparrow?" he growls, his fingers biting into my wrists and his body grinding deep. "Is this what your tight little cunt needs?"

"Yes!" I cry out, arching up to meet him, because fuck, it is. The brutal thrust of his body, his suffocating weight and the wild grunts he sounds.

It thrills me. Deep down, in that dark shameful place where my desire twists tighter, craving and raw, I'm ready, I want to be owned. Possessed.

By him.

Sebastian yanks me closer, shoving my legs up over his shoulders, almost folding me in two. "Such a wet little whore," he groans, pistoning his cock into me again, and fuck, this new angle makes me cry out, clutching blindly at the sheets.

So good. Right there. Fuck.

I scream.

"That's right, baby. Scream for daddy." Sebastian roars, keeping up his merciless pace. "Scream for this cock like you mean it."

"Yes! Please! *Fuck...*"

Sebastian suddenly pulls out and flips me over, so I'm down on all fours on the bed. I barely have time to lift my face from the pillows and suck in a breath before he mounts me like a fucking animal, shoving his cock in deep from behind as he grabs a fistful of my hair.

"You're mine now," he growls, pulling me back, flush against him. His breath is hot in my ear as his cock thrusts up inside me. "I'm fucking branding you, from the inside out.

This body, these sweet breasts, this tight little cunt. They're mine."

Oh God.

I'm whimpering now, mindless with the pleasure that's building, cresting deep inside me. Sebastian yanks at my hair, painful. "Who do you belong to?" he demands.

I sob, my body jolting with the force of his wild thrusts.

"Who? Say it!"

His hand closes around my throat. Squeezing. *Fuck, yes.*

"You!" I scream, as my body goes limp in his arms, the surrender sweeping through me like a tidal wave. "I'm yours. Only yours!"

"That's my good girl."

My orgasm comes upon me so fast that I can't even brace myself for the onslaught of it. Every muscle in my body spasms in pure ecstasy, and I scream. Over and over, babbling his name in delirious pleasure as I'm wrecked. Ravaged.

Totally undone.

I feel Sebastian's cock grind up deep inside me, his grip stutter, and then he pulls out, shoving me face-down on the bed. I collapse willingly, reeling as he comes with a roar, hot liquid spilling over my back, coating me.

Marking me.

I lay there in a haze of pleasure, utterly spent. My body aches in the best ways, and my mind is still just a blur. Distantly, I feel Sebastian return, and clean me up with a damp cloth before tucking the covers around me, and slipping into bed beside me, a heavy arm pulling me into the spoon of his body.

The lights go out. His breathing slows beside me. As I lay there, wide awake in bed beside him.

My heart breaking in my chest.

Finally, his body stills. He's asleep.

I slip out of the bed, and tiptoe across the room to the door. My heart is racing with every step, until I'm safely down the hallway, and in my room.

I sob.

Not with pleasure, this time, or desperate desire, but the aching, empty knowledge that there's no going back.

Because Sebastian was right, he does own me now—a precious part that I can never take back from him. Not the mythical idea of my virginity, but something worse.

Those moments of pure emotion that just passed between us, in the midst of passion. My trust.

My submission.

Tears stinging in my eyes, I go over to the dresser. Pulling open the top drawer, I reach underneath it and feel for the locket I taped to the underside. It was probably silly to even bring it with me, but I somehow knew that I might need a reminder of why I'm doing this.

I open the locket and stare down at Miles's face inside. The photo torn and frayed at the edges. Fading now, like the memories of our time together.

"I'm sorry," I whisper, aching with pain and regret. "I'm so, so sorry."

I hate myself for what I just did.

But I have to hate Sebastian more. At least until this is over.

I *will* destroy him, even if I destroy myself, too.

Chapter 22

Avery

I wake early, after a restless night of shame and self-loathing. Pulling on workout gear, I leave a message with Leon downstairs, and head out on an early-morning run through the silent streets.

I need to clear my head—and my heart.

I cried myself to sleep last night thinking about Miles and everything that's brought me here. But my dreams were filled with fantasies of Sebastian. Memories, too, of his hands. His body.

His cock, thrusting deep inside.

I wish I could block it all out, but my traitorous body is still humming with sensation, sore, and reminding me with every step how completely Sebastian laid claim to me.

Because I begged him to.

And if I'd hoped that finally offering up my virginity would somehow cleanse me of this intoxicating sexual attraction that I feel for him ... Well, I know I failed. Because the sex last night wasn't just epic and pleasurable, fulfilling my darkest fantasies of submission.

It was a connection, too.

Raw and real, some inexplicable bond between me and Sebastian. Like my defenses crumbled, and he, in turn, was allowing me to glimpse some hidden side of him, too. Sweet, tender, caring.

All the things I thought he didn't have the heart to be.

But now I've seen them, I can't shake that knowledge. Sebastian is capable of feeling, of love and loyalty, too—that much is clear from his relationship with his sister. He proved it with the way he spoke to her, and the hollow guilt in his eyes when he told me about trying to protect her...

I have to give a bitter laugh as I suddenly realize: The weakness I've been searching for?

It's Scarlett.

He cares about something. Or rather, *someone*. But my stomach churns at the idea of using Scarlett against him. She's an innocent, who's already suffered enough.

What happened to being merciless?

What happened to avenging Miles' death, no matter what the cost?

I'm torn. I can't waver in my mission, but surely there has to be a line that I won't cross?

But isn't that what Sebastian counts on? Other people's morality holding them back, making them meek, while he never compromises.

Never once questions the collateral damage it takes to bring about his utter domination.

I turn the question over in my mind, running a long loop through the park until my body is exhausted. Finally, I head back to the house.

I don't know what to expect. I've never done the 'morning after' thing with anyone. How will Sebastian react to me now?

Will he prove everyone right, and lose all interest in me now the thrill of the chase is over, and he's claimed his prize?

Or did he feel the connection between us too? Something deeper than just our bodies craving release...

I find myself nervous with anticipation as I let myself in and climb the stairs to my room. I need another shower before I face him, and the defense of another demure outfit. Something pretty to remind me of the fact I'm still playing a role for him, and I can't let my guard slip again, even for a minute. Maybe the cream dress, I muse, mentally running through my new designer wardrobe. Or the blue—

"There you are."

I startle at the sight of Sebastian, standing like a statue in the middle of the room. "Hi!" I blurt, my pulse racing—from the surprise, and the sight of him again, after all the intimacy we shared last night.

He's dressed for work, in a crisp shirt and well cut suit, his physique even more impressive now that I know how that body feels, pinning me to the mattress.

Then I see his face, and my heart stops in my chest.

It's empty. Cold. As remote as I've ever seen him.

"It's so nice out, I thought I'd take a run," I continue nervously. I look around, wondering what the hell is going on. Something is very wrong here. "Did you want to grab some breakfast?"

Sebastian doesn't say a word, he just holds out his hand to me. It's balled in a fist, and slowly, he opens it to reveal what he's holding.

My locket dangles from his fingertips.

The locket with Miles' photo inside. A man I should have no way of knowing.

My blood turns to ice, fear shivering through me in an instant.

"Who the fuck are you?" Sebastian demands, his words laced with rage.

I can see the betrayal in his eyes now, and I feel an unwelcome pang. But that's just crazy, I have no reason to feel guilty for lying to him. He's the villain here. The monster.

And now he's coming for me.

I back up, anxious. I need to get the hell out of here.

"Tell me!" Sebastian roars, pacing closer. "The truth, dammit. What the hell is this? What's going on?"

I don't reply.

Instead, I grab my bag from beside the door, and race out of the room, heading down the stairs. Sebastian powers after me, catching up just as I reach the front door.

He slams it shut, blocking my path.

Fuck.

I gather all my strength and look him in the eye. "Move," I order him, even as I'm quaking inside. I didn't plan for this. *Fuck*, why didn't I plan for this?

Because I was foolish. I thought I could beat the monster at his own game. But looking at Sebastian now, consumed with rage and fury, I can see, I'm in way over my head.

I have no weapons. No friends. Nobody to call.

"Get out of my way," I repeat, growing more desperate. "You can't keep me here!"

Sebastian lets out a cruel laugh. "You want to leave? Fine." He steps aside. "But there's only one place you're going. At least, until I have my answers."

I barrel past him, outside—

And find a white medical van blocking the driveway. Three men in scrubs are waiting. They advance, approaching me.

What the hell is going on?

"She's unstable, please be careful," Sebastian says from behind me.

I turn in time to see a smug look on his face, before one of the men grabs for me.

"No!" I yell, kicking out with pure instinct. I make contact with his shin, and hear him curse, before another one grabs me from behind. "Let me go! What are you doing?" I yell, struggling in panic. I manage to slash at this guy's face with my nails and make a break for it.

But I don't get far. There are too many of them, surrounding me, dragging me to the ground and pinning me face-down, my hands yanked painfully behind my back.

"Let go of me!" I yell, shaking in fear, but they ignore me. I'm bound with some kind of zip tie, and hauled to my feet, dragged towards the back of the van. "You can't do this!"

But they can.

"Stop!" I scream, but no one listens. I'm half-carried, half-dragged into the van, and strapped down to some kind of stretcher, binding snapping shut at my ankles and around my waist.

I struggle, but it's in vain. I can't move. I can't run.

I'm trapped.

Sebastian strolls closer. "You can see, she's in quite a state," he calmly says to one of the men. "She's a risk to herself and others."

"Let me go!" I howl, but they ignore me.

"Don't worry, Mr. Wolfe," the man nods. "We'll give her a full psychiatric evaluation."

That's when I see the writing printed on the scrubs of the man nearest to me.

Larkspur.

Oh God.

The place they sent Scarlett. The one Sebastian himself

described as pure hell. He's sending me there? Panic consumes me, and I gasp for air.

"You bastard!" I scream, still struggling with everything I have. "How could you?"

Sebastian is walking back to the house, but he stops at my ragged cry. He turns, and slowly strolls back to the van, leaning in through the open doors, so his face is just inches from mine.

Cruel. Cold.

The monster I always knew he was.

"Nobody fucks with me." Sebastian says slowly. Calmly. "Whoever you really are, you'll rue the day you tried to take me on. No one is coming for you. Your life is in my hands now. And I will get my answers."

He backs up and the door slams closed. The engine starts.

I'm still reeling, strapped to the stretcher, when I feel a sharp prick in my arm. I turn my head to find one of the orderlies emptying a syringe into me. I struggle and writhe, but it's no use.

Sebastian's right.

Nobody is coming for me—because nobody knows I'm in trouble. My secret mission has backfired in the worst possible way. There's no hope, no way to talk my way out of this.

I came here to destroy him, but I'm Sebastian's captive now.

TO BE CONTINUED...

What happens next? Avery and Sebastian's twisted love story continues in Priceless Secret - available now!

Revenge. They say it will drive a man out of his mind. But what about a woman? We're supposed to be the fairer sex. Gentle.

Forgiving.

But there's nothing forgiving about the oath I swore: I'm going to destroy Sebastian Wolfe. Even if it costs me everything.

My innocence. My life.

My *heart.*

But what if the line between love and hate breaks forever?

The Priceless Trilogy:

PRICELESS: BOOK TWO
PRICELESS SECRET

Revenge. They say it will drive a man out of his mind. But what about a woman? We're supposed to be the fairer sex. Gentle.

Forgiving.

But there's nothing forgiving about the oath I swore: I'm going to destroy Sebastian Wolfe. Even if it costs me everything.

My innocence. My life.

My *heart*.

But what if the line between love and hate breaks forever?

The Priceless Trilogy:
1. Priceless Kiss (Sebastian & Avery)
2. Priceless Secret (Sebastian & Avery)
3. Priceless Fate (Sebastian & Avery)

Roxy Sloane is a USA Today bestselling author, with over 2 million books sold world-wide. She loves writing page-turning spicy romance full of captivatingly alpha heroes, sensual passion, and a sprinkle of glamor. She lives in Los Angeles, and enjoys shocking whoever looks at her laptop screen when she writes in local coffee shops.

* * *

To get free books, news and more, sign up to my VIP list!

www.roxysloane.com
roxy@roxysloane.com